CABIN 1

STEELE SHADOWS SECURITY

AMANDA MCKINNEY

HH TISEVICH

Paperback ISBN 978-1-7340133-1-3
eBook ISBN 978-1-7324635-9-2

Editor(s): Nancy Brown
Cover Design: Steamy Reads Designs

Amanda
MCKINNEY
AUTHOR OF SEXY MURDER MYSTERIES

https://www.amandamckinneyauthor.com

DEDICATION

For Mama, always, and forever and ever.

A special and very heartfelt thank you to my editor and awesome team of Beta Readers – Nancy, Irene, Peggy, Becca, Metzi, Sue, Stephen, Diane, and Robin. I owe it all to you for creating the best story possible for my readers. Thank you, thank you, thank you!

A note from the author:

Welcome to the small, southern town of Berry Springs! If you're looking for sizzling-hot alpha males, smart, independent females, and page-turning mystery, you've come to the right place. As you might have guessed, STEELE SHADOWS SECURITY is a spin-off series from the Berry Springs Series. But don't worry, you don't need to read Berry Springs first. Think of Steele Shadows as Berry Springs' darker, grittier, bad boy brother. That said, grab a tall glass of sweet tea (or vodka if you're feeling saucy), and settle in for a fun adventure that—I hope—gives you a little escape from the day to day... (and maybe a little crush on the Steele brothers).

Enjoy!

ALSO BY AMANDA MCKINNEY

Lethal Legacy

The Woods (A Berry Springs Novel)

The Lake (A Berry Springs Novel)

The Storm (A Berry Springs Novel)

The Fog (A Berry Springs Novel)

The Creek (A Berry Springs Novel)

The Shadow (A Berry Springs Novel)

The Cave (A Berry Springs Novel)

Devil's Gold (A Black Rose Mystery, Book 1)

Hatchet Hollow (A Black Rose Mystery, Book 2)

Tomb's Tale (A Black Rose Mystery Book 3)

Evil Eye (A Black Rose Mystery Book 4)

Sinister Secrets (A Black Rose Mystery Book 5)

#1 BESTSELLING SERIES:

Cabin 1 (Steele Shadows Security)

Cabin 2 (Steele Shadows Security)

Cabin 3 (Steele Shadows Security)

Phoenix (Steele Shadows Rising)

Jagger (Steele Shadows Investigations)

Ryder (Steele Shadows Investigations)

★*Rattlesnake Road, coming Spring 2021* ★
★*Redemption Road, coming Summer 2021* ★

And many more to come...

AWARDS AND RECOGNITION

THE STORM
Winner of the 2018 Golden Leaf for Romantic Suspense
2018 Maggie Award for Excellence Finalist
2018 Silver Falchion Finalist
2018 Beverley Finalist
2018 Passionate Plume Honorable Mention Recipient

THE FOG
Winner of the 2019 Golden Quill for Romantic Suspense
Winner of the 2019 I Heart Indie Award for Romantic Suspense
2019 Maggie Award of Excellence Finalist
2019 Stiletto Award Finalist

CABIN 1 (STEELE SHADOWS SECURITY)
2020 National Readers Choice Award Finalist
2020 HOLT Medallion Finalist

THE CAVE
2020 Book Buyers Best Finalist
2020 Carla Crown Jewel Finalist

DIRTY BLONDE

2017 2nd Place Winner for It's a Mystery Contest

"**The Woods** is a sexy, small-town murder mystery that's guaranteed to resonate with fans of Nora Roberts and Karin Slaughter." -Best Thrillers

"Danger, mystery, and sizzling-hot romance right down to the last page." -Amazon Review, **The Creek**

"A dark, ominous thrilling tale spiked with a dash of romance and mystery that captivated me from start to finish..." -The Coffeeholic Bookworm, **The Lake**

"**The Storm** is a beautifully written whodunnit, packed with suspense, danger, and hot romance. Kept me guessing who the murderer was. I couldn't put it down!" -Amazon Review

"I devoured **The Cave** in one sitting. Best one yet." -Amazon Review

"**The Shadow** is a suspense-filled, sexy as hell book." -Bookbub Review

Fair Warning: Cabin 1 contains adult language, content, and steamy love scenes. Just FYI.

LET'S CONNECT!

Text **AMANDABOOKS to 66866** to sign up
for Amanda's Newsletter and get the latest
on new releases, promos, and freebies! Or, sign up below.

Amanda
MCKINNEY
AUTHOR OF SEXY MURDER MYSTERIES

https://www.amandamckinneyauthor.com

CABIN 1

Hidden deep in the remote mountains of Berry Springs is a private security firm where some go to escape, and others find exactly what they've been looking for.

Welcome to Cabin 1, Cabin 2, Cabin 3...

Cocky, reckless, and die-hard playboy are just a few of the names Gage Steele has been called since he left the Marines and moved back to the small, southern town of Berry Springs to take over his father's security firm. On the one-year anniversary of his father's death, Gage has only two things in mind—endless whiskey and endless women. What he got was a battered, bruised spitfire stumbling through the woods in the middle of the night.

Newly-appointed prosecutor and unapologetic workaholic, Niki Avery has spent her life working toward one goal—never to have to depend on anyone but herself... until the day she gets brutally attacked on the side of the road. Stripped of her Louis Vuitton and her dignity, the fiercely independent ADA must submit to being under the watchful eye of a former Marine, a loose cannon with a temper as scorching as his looks.

As cracks begin to show in the Steele family, including newly discovered evidence that their father's death was no accident, Gage wrestles with his growing feelings for his client, knowing not only that Niki is off-limits, but together, they were like gasoline and fire—an explosion he wanted nothing more than to ignite in the bedroom. But when a pair of bloody body parts show up at the compound, it becomes clear that Niki's attacker hasn't given up and Gage realizes he'll do anything to keep her safe... even as his own family is spiraling out of control.

1

NIKI

*D*arkness swallowed me as a cloud drifted over the full moon, taking my sight along with it. I didn't stop.

I couldn't stop.

Rocks, sticks, and God knew what else cut into the bottom of my feet as they flew over the rocky terrain. *Thump, thump, thump* against the dead leaves and pine needles scattered on the forest floor. I couldn't see a thing, so I focused on the sounds around me—but even that was drowned out by my hammering heartbeat and gasping breaths.

The woods at night. Magical, alluring, still. No, not that night. That night it was a thinly veiled evil, a muted witness to my death if I were to get caught. That night, the woods were my escape, my refuge, my only chance for survival.

The clouds shifted, a silver glow washing over the mountains, casting shadows along the ground like ghosts swaying back and forth. I blinked, adjusting, and heaved myself over the boulder I was about to slam into. My body tumbled to the ground like a sack of potatoes, the breath knocking out of my lungs when I hit the cold, wet dirt.

I froze, my eyes shooting open.

Did he see me? Hear me?

Holding my breath, I flattened against the ground, my heart a thundering staccato. I focused on the moon above me, like a spotlight hellbent on pinpointing my location. A breeze whistled through the trees, the almost-bare branches moving like slashes through the moon.

Dead leaves, dead trees. Autumn in the mountains had never looked so haunting. Or been so cold.

Snick.

My eyes widened in terror. I willed myself to fade into the night, into the ground—fitting, considering that's where he wanted to put me.

I didn't blink, didn't breathe as the seconds ticked by.

Had I lost him?

A rustle of leaves had my pulse kickstarting into panic mode again.

I knew I couldn't stay there.

I stayed, I died. That simple truth had me gritting my teeth, forcing myself off the ground and taking off again, pushing into a sprint once more.

Branches sliced my skin as I ran blindly through the pitch-black forest with only slivers of light cutting through the thick canopy of trees to guide my way. I had no idea where I was, no idea where I was going. All I knew was that forward was my only option. My only option to preserve the life that he wanted so badly to take away. So badly to ravage, control, and use like a blow up doll with a bottle of lube. As if that was all I was worth. As if the thirty-three years I'd lived on this planet were worth nothing. As if my entire life had led to that moment. *To him.* The life that the last thirty minutes had rewritten in the cold hard scripture of sexual assault.

You want to know the kicker of it? I wasn't sad, defeated, crippled by fear or sudden depression. No, I was *pissed*. Infuriated. An indescribable rage for the two men who thought they could treat me like that. The two men who thought they could take everything away from me.

Screw. That.

I hadn't stopped shaking, deep from within the confines of that newfound fury coursing through my veins like speed. Fury... and perhaps an adrenaline rush from killing one of them.

I'd stopped wiping the blood from my face when I was certain that *my* blood had washed *his* away from my skin.

His blood.

His blood that had sprayed me like a tortured artist madly flicking paint against his canvas, an upward sweeping motion designed to let me know I'd hit my target. Although, truthfully, there was no target. Only an animalistic need for survival that overtook all else. A desire to live. A power that came from somewhere else... somewhere I hoped to God I never had to pull from again. A switch had flipped inside me. A switch that if I wouldn't have had, I'd be lying in a bloody heap in the middle of a ditch, dissolved to nothing more than scavenger bait.

I was always a cautious woman. I'd taken self-defense, never ran with headphones, always carried a shiv in the hem of my leggings. Alert, ready, even a few times playing out an attack in my head, imagining what I would do, and how I would defend myself. I *would* defend myself, I knew, with the brute force that my skinny arms, legs, hands could provide. That would be enough, right?

Then, it happened. All those badass fictional Jolie

fighter scenes I'd created were thrown out the window in seconds flat. Truth is, there's nothing to prepare you for it. The moment they pinned me to the wet, moldy, dirty ground, I surprised myself. I told myself I wasn't going to be a victim. I wasn't going to let these bastards take anything from me. *Nothing.* I was going to fight, and fight until death if I had too.

I'd made the decision.

They both wore ski masks, the knitted ones with only cut-outs for the eyes and mouth. They'd run me off the road and jumped out, guns blazing, and with the cold steel of a pistol pointed between my eyes, ordered me out of my vehicle. I offered my purse, wallet, even my brand-new Jeep. Nope—they ordered me out, and looking back, that's when I knew. That's when I knew that dollar bills and credit cards weren't what they wanted. No, these bastards wanted something much more sacred. Much more valued.

I'd tried to gas it, only digging my tires deeper into the muddy ditch where they'd run me off the road.

Worst case scenario.

"Never get out of your car"... the common sense warning echoed in my brain as they screamed at me, hyped up on booze, drugs, whatever. I'd gripped the steering wheel, frozen like a statue as the words repeated in my head.

Never get out of your car.

Unfortunately, all that well-meaning advice didn't do much for me when they opened the door and dragged me out by my hair. I knew screaming wouldn't help, but I tried anyway, desperate to let them know I wasn't going to bend over and take it without a fight. That I wasn't some weakling dissolved to tears. No, I screamed. So loud I thought my vocal cords were going to pop.

A punch in the side of the face silenced that real quick.

I looked up at their cheap black ski masks, the kind you'd find at any discount retail shop, which led me to my first clue about them—they were walking clichés, a pair of assholes that had watched one too many cheesy scary movies. I would've had more respect for them if they'd shown me their faces. Do me like a real man. Not a man who had to use violence to get it, had to have the flow of liquor running through his veins before he got the balls enough to attack. Like a man so weak he couldn't control his impulses, couldn't overcome the natural human instinct to take what he wanted. Not strong enough. No, these two were nothing but cowards. *That*... that's what gave me the courage to fight.

I'd thrashed on the ground as they ripped at my clothes, kicking, punching, scratching. Spittle from the fat one's mouth dripped onto my face, panting, panting, panting like a dog in heat. I kept fighting but two drunk, horny, grown men with adrenaline highs were tough to fight off. The fat one stunk. Like rancid B.O., cheap cologne, and cheap booze.

The skinnier one that had punched me had stepped back at that point, watching it all unfold. Staring down at me like a piece of trash. Waiting his turn. I swore I could see him smiling through the mask.

For whatever reason, I hated him more than the fat bastard on top of me. The skinny one had gone eerily calm. *Knew* what he was doing.

I didn't stop fighting, even with a knife to my neck, I kept wrestling with the fat one... until another blow to the face blinded me. I was dazed, slipping in and out of consciousness like some first-timer at a frat party. I remember my hearing going in and out, the dark forest around me suddenly silent.

That was my first real twinge of fear. My instinct telling me that I was in real trouble.

I blinked, willing the waves of nausea to subside, focusing on the blanket of trees above me and the beams of moonlight piercing through the darkness onto my face.

I remember a bright red leaf flittering down from the tree above me. I watched it, fixated on it, in some hypnotic state as he began pulling down my shorts.

Slowly, catching in the breeze, the leaf drifted through the air, sparkling in the moonlight. So soft, gentle, a beautiful fire-red marking its peak of life before falling to the ground to shrivel up and die.

I was that leaf.

But I wasn't going to die.

I'll never forget that moment, the moment the cool autumn air swept over my bare skin. The vulnerability that came with it.

The *hate.* Oh, God, the hatred toward these men.

It was *that* hate that saved my life.

The moment the fat one reached down to undo his ripped, dirty, knockoff designer jeans—I took the chance. Kneed the bastard in the balls and ripped the knife from his hand, shredding mine in the process. With a guttural scream, I shoved the blade into his neck.

The world stopped.

His eyes froze with shock as the knife went in. The stun —the one, single moment of vulnerability in his eyes as the blade severed his carotid artery. Then the eyes... oh, God, how his eyes glazed over as he went limp and fell on top of me, half his body on me, the other half next to the shirt and bra they'd ripped off me.

Next to what would be the moments that changed my

life forever. The moments that brutally ripped every last shred of dignity away from me.

The moment that I, Niki Avery, killed a man.

Murdered another human being.

That's when the skinny one turned and ran back to his truck. Like the dirtbag he was, he was going to take off.

That's what I'd thought anyway.

I didn't immediately roll the guy off me and jump up, as you might think I would. Instead, I laid there, chest heaving, staring up at the sky as the last few seconds settled around me, the sweet, metallic scent of blood filling the air. I swore I could hear it pumping out of his fat neck. I didn't want to look over, I didn't want to see it.

The pain started to wave through my body as the blood in my mouth began to register, the knots on my face beginning to throb. Arms, feeling like a thousand pieces of glass had shredded them. I raised my head first, my eyes locking on that leaf. That damn red leaf that had flittered onto my stomach.

We won, I thought, as I rolled the dead man off me, then plucked the leaf from my stomach and grabbed my clothes now saturated in blood.

The headlights of my Jeep grotesquely illuminated the man I'd just killed, lying there on the ground, his head encircled in a growing puddle of blood, his eyes open and staring directly at me, the whites reflecting in the beam of light.

I knew that image would haunt me for the rest of my life.

I was right.

Movement caught my eye and I was pulled out of my weird daze. The skinny one didn't leave. No, he was standing over me, calmly, terrifying, with a gun pointed directly at my face.

Run was my only thought.

Run.

So I did.

I kicked rocks into his face, then like a cannonball out of a rocket I hurled myself over the dead body as the *pop* of the gun blasted behind me. Scrambling to pull up my shorts, I stumbled into the woods, ice-cold fear sending my pulse spinning, and one shoe into the air. Maybe it was the adrenaline crashing, or the emotional aftershock of taking a life, but the cage-fighter inside me was gone.

I was scared.

Out of my mind scared.

My heart thundered, the realization that I was out in the middle of freaking nowhere hit me like a metal bat. I heard the snapping of twigs behind me.

The bastard was chasing me.

I pushed harder, faster, gasping for breath as I navigated the uneven terrain, running deeper into the mountains.

I'd kept running, running, running, switching directions, weaving in and out of the trees like a gazelle attempting to throw off the lion behind her. I'd changed directions, even switched back a few times. Kept running, running, even when the heavy footsteps behind me had faded.

That lasted for hours—*hours*—until I finally let myself stop.

I was left lost, bruised, broken, covered in blood and disgust somewhere in the vast mountains of Berry Springs.

2

GAGE

*T*hey say the only easy day is yesterday. Fuck that. It had been a year since I'd left the Marines, MARSOC to be exact. One year of late mornings, booze, women, and more women. The life of waking up in the middle of bumfuck nowhere with a seven-inch centipede nibbling on my ball sack moments before a welcoming committee of bullets rained down on me were long gone. One year ago, my life was the mission—I was taught to eat, sleep, drink the mission. Ask questions later. On second thought, don't ask questions at all. See, I never was good at following orders. That medal of conformity went to my twin brother, Axel. The star Steele. The perfect one. He was always the good twin, the top of his class, the leader of the mission. Me? Nope, I was the screw up. Always pushing the boundaries, never settling for the status quo. Always asking too many questions. Call me crazy—and believe me, some have—but I liked to know who's eyes I was putting a bullet between. I liked to know why I assassinated the leader of one of the many shitholes in the desert. I liked to know why I bombed a house-full of children, then woke up the next morning to the spin on the news blaming the explosion on the latest and greatest radical group. Missions go right, missions go wrong. Lives saved; lives lost. Hell of a way to live. A mix of chaos and order sure to screw with any man's head. But all that bullshit was behind me now. All I needed now was a bottle of Jack, a few rounds in the ring with whichever of my brothers dared to go up against K.O.—that was my nickname in the military. Never lost a fight, never let the other asshole remember it. Yep, all I needed was a good fight followed by a few rounds at the range with my HK416.

Well, that and a willing blonde with a tight ass and solid southern accent.

They say the only easy day is yesterday... that night, my plan was to be carried to my bed on the cushion of a nice pair of fake titties and lay like a limp fish while she had her way with me, while I drifted off into oblivion. A place I'd become very familiar with over the last year.

That night, I drank to forget.

The universe had other plans for me.

I flicked my wrist to the bartender, Suzie, who was wearing a low-cut tank-top, that may, or may not, have had a tiny hole at the bottom of her left breast. One-hundred percent cotton rarely held up against a stretch like that. Double D's if I had to guess, although I'd found myself surprised over the last year. Damn padded bras take the fun out of everything.

She smiled, a blush coloring her cheeks. I fought the grin back—always nice to know my skills were appreciated. I watched her as she got waylaid by a trio of rough-and-tumble cowboys, a walking cliché in Frank's Bar, a tavern located on the outskirts of town. I can still remember the first time I snuck through the back door of Frank's, stole his only bottle of Johnnie Walker Blue, then drank the entire thing while wandering the vast mountains of Berry Springs. Ax found me the next day passed out under a pine tree in a puddle of my own vomit, with a smile on my face. Twin ESP, he called it. I called him my guardian angel. Claimed my pants were down, with a mysterious slime snaking around my body and claw marks on the tree trunk. Don't take everything Ax says at face value, there's your advice of the day. Anyway, it was months before I could look at a bottle of anything with pure grain alcohol.

And months before the rash went away. Still don't know what the fuck got me that night, but I'd sure like to find it again.

I sat back and watched the cowboys, listened to the boisterous laughter as they ordered another round. PBR, I'd bet my life on it. Based on their Stetsons and cologne to match, I guessed they were out looking to round up some fine country ass. Not much different than I, but based on the empty pitchers in front of them, whoever they conned to take home was in for a jarring disappointment of whiskey dick.

Whiskey dick never was a problem with me. If anything, the amber liquid gave me powers second only to Zeus. Fuck that, I'd measure against the Greek God any day of the week.

They ordered a round of tequila shots—*shocker*—then Suzie settled her attention back on me. My head tilted as she walked over, keeping my eye on that potential peep show. I felt her eyes boring into me, felt that feline smile spreading across her face. She didn't care that I was staring. She sure as hell didn't the other night.

"I'd say 'take a picture, it'll last longer', but this isn't a nineties rom com."

Yep. Tiny hole. Red lace bra.

Nice.

I shifted in my seat, feeling a zing of primal lust. My goal that night was to drink to forget... only after a roll in the sack with that red bra. I tore my eyes away from the watermelons in front of me and met her chocolate brown ones with a wink. "Rom com, huh? I was thinking about another kind of film..."

Those eyes sparkled as she leaned in on her forearms, her breasts plumping up like hot air balloons. "Was thinking the same thing, sugar. I get off in two hours—"

"Ah, *Suz,* good to see you."

My impending boner was crushed by the bear-claw squeeze on my shoulder. I turned to see my older brother, Phoenix—Feen for short—and his icy expression lacing into my temptation of the evening. *Stay the hell away from my brother,* he might as well have said out loud.

Suzie recoiled like a whipped dog. Phoenix tended to have that effect on women. Then again, we all did if the mood struck us. Six-foot-three former special-ops Marines trained in lethal combat had that tendency on people.

She straightened, turned back to me, her boobs falling back in place—dammit. "Another whiskey?" The sparkle in those eyes long gone.

"Yep, and Hulk here will take one too." I slid Feen the side-eye. "Make his a double." My attention was pulled to another ring of drunken laughter from the end of the bar. "Who are those guys?"

Suzie rolled her eyes. "Don't know two of them, but the big one's Butch. Regular here. Big hunter. Rowdy, rude, with the temper of a rattlesnake. Asshole."

"So you're saying you two dated." I winked.

She snorted. "Not on your life. I'll get those drinks."

Suzie walked away and Feen shifted his fuck-you expression to the trucker next to me. Six feet, solid muscle, with a

Ruger hidden under his oversized flannel shirt. I couldn't fight the small grin that crossed my lips when the redneck grabbed his beer and slid out of his seat—as if he was about to leave anyway. *Yeah right.* Like I said, Feen had that effect on people.

Feen settled in next to me. I focused on the mirrored back wall lined with liquor bottles.

"How long you been here?" He asked.

I glanced at my watch, fighting the angel-devil thing. It was already nine o'clock... or was it ten?

"Don't lie to me."

Angel it is, then. "Since seven."

Suzie delivered the drinks ice-cold, *and ice-cold,* confirming that my brother blew any chance I had of swinging from that red lace bra later that night.

I threw back my drink.

Feen wrapped his hands around his, focusing on the amber liquid as if it were a crystal ball. Similarly, I settled my gaze on the sparkling liquor bottles as if they were my savior.

A heavy minute passed with each of us avoiding the elephant in the room, as we all had done so exquisitely the last year.

The over-protective oldest Steele brother caved first.

"How you doin'?" He sipped.

I kept my eyes on the whiskey bottle with the blue label, willing it to magically refill my shot glass. No luck.

"Fine," I said, knowing he didn't believe it.

"Heard you out at the range this afternoon."

I cocked my brow and looked at him, waiting for...

"Then, I picked up the empty beer cans and whiskey bottle in your room."

There it was.

I shook my head. Feen was predictable if nothing else.

"Listen, give me a break, alright? I don't have a client right now..." And it was the one fucking year anniversary of Dad's death, you asswipe.

Feen sipped his drink, knowing he'd ruffled my feathers, and that was his intention. Nag me enough to where I'd finally bend over and say, 'fine, I'll quit drinking.'

I waited for him to go in hard, instead, he switched subjects on me.

"Jagg sent us a mother and kid today. The dad beat them up. Beat them both up. Guy got out on bail, and Jagg brought them to us."

Jagg was the nickname we'd given our buddy and military brother, Max Jagger, a former Navy SEAL turned detective for the state criminal investigations division. A good friend to have when you ran a private security business.

Feen continued, "I'm having Celeste set them up with fake identities, the whole nine yards. They'll be with us at least a few days."

"Are you giving them to me?" A flicker of excitement sent my spine straightening. Finally something to do. It hadn't been lost on me that the unofficial CEO of our family business had been tossing me a bunch of busy work the last few weeks.

Feen slowly turned his sweating glass around in his hands. My stomach got that nervous twinge as I searched his face, awaiting whatever the hell he was about to lay down on me. I knew that look. I knew it well.

"It's been a year, brother," he said. "You've had your time to process. It's enough."

"What's *enough*, exactly?"

"The drinking. The girls. Shit, Gage, we run a private security firm for Christ's sake. You've got Celeste working overtime vetting every woman you bring through the back door—"

"Back door's the best—"

"Quit it, Gage, I'm serious. And I'm sick of wanting a drink at the end of the day, and all the fucking booze has been lapped up. It's enough, Gage."

The heat rose to my neck. *You're too defensive, Gage, too hotheaded for your own good,* my Dad's words echoed in my ear. Dad might've been right, and hell, Phoenix might have been right, but *I* decide. I made the decisions in my life. I decided my own missions.

So what did I do then? Raised my hand and ordered another round. In his face.

"I might need to lay off the booze, Feen, but you need to relax the fuck up. Maybe a few nights with a few women is what you need. A few at the same time, even. Ever tried that? Forget the back door..." Suzie delivered my drink and I took a sip. "When was the last time you even talked to what's-her-name? That red-haired waitress from Donny's."

"Amber."

"Of course."

"Eleven months."

I spit my whiskey on the table, earning a few glances from across the room. Like I gave a shit.

"Don't tell me it's been that long since you've had sex."

"We all deal with shit differently. Besides, you've been having enough sex for all of us, Gage."

Anger, defensiveness, whatever, grabbed me around the neck. I snapped back. "I'm the first one up at the compound, doing a perimeter check. Drunk or not. I handle my business, Feen. It's not like I'm out blowing our billion dollar inheritance. Like I'd like to be, honestly. So what if I like booze and women?" I lifted my open palms. "Just trying to spread some love in the fucking shadow of darkness that lingers around the place."

"You writing a poem?"

"Fuck you."

"You're going to be spreading a lot more if you're not careful."

"I'm always careful."

Feen nodded, a grin cracking his face. "True, I guess. Celeste has started recycling your condom wrappers."

I laughed.

Feen blew out a breath and took another sip, a deep sip, and I watched his shoulders start to relax. He continued, "Anyway, you're not getting the family with the abusive dad. I'm giving them to Gunner. You're going to clean your shit up before you get another client, got it?"

"That's bullshit, Feen."

"Listen, Gage, I have no doubt in my mind you could take the family on, and we wouldn't have to worry about a thing. We handle our business, that's what we do. Always have. Something else we do? Call each other out. Watch out for each other. That's what families do. I'll be damned if I watch you drink your life away because of something we can't control. There, I'm calling you out. And I'm going to make sure it's taken care of."

"Fine. Less women."

"Less *booze,* Gage."

"Now, that's just asking too much." I smiled in an attempt to lighten the damn mood. Feen wasn't entertained, so I continued, "I've handled Dad's death with booze. You? You've turned into a neurotic, paranoid shitshow, you know that?"

"Someone has to run the business."

"I've told you... hell, we've *all* told you, you don't have to carry it all. You have three other brothers, Feen. We can split up the workload. Just because you're the first born doesn't mean you have to take over everything."

He lifted his hand and wagged his fingers. "Well, let's see, then... which of my brothers can handle it? Let's see how we've all changed since we got that damn call..." He lifted one finger, "You? You're a womanizing drunk. Ax? Guy's pretty much disappeared. Become a freaking hermit. And Gunner? That ball of pent up rage spends every second down at the range target shooting."

All true. All four of us had left the military to pick up the pieces when our Dad died. In an instant, we had more money than we could spend in ten lifetimes and also became owners of one of the top private security firms in the country, with employees and clients all over the world. In an instant, four guys who could handle anything on the battlefield, turned into a cluster fuck of messes, trying to adapt to their new lives.

Running a damn business.

I sighed. "What about Dallas?"

"She does her part. Hell, she's running the estates, handling the personnel... she's doing more than her part. I'm not going to ask her to take on more with the business. You know Dad, anyway, he always let her do her own thing."

"She wouldn't have it any other way."

Feen snorted. Dallas, our stepmom of fifteen years, once the wife of a billionaire, now a grieving widow.

Suzie sauntered back by. We watched her coolly. I was no longer interested in that hole in her shirt. Feen was a buzz kill like no other. After she left, Feen leaned in.

"You're always after the damsel in distress, Gage."

"What about that," I nodded to the soaring peaks under Suzie's shirt, "says damsel in distress?"

"I mean, you're always after the girls who need something, who're looking for someone, or someone to take care of them. You need to meet someone who challenges you. Someone who has their own life, their own thing."

I watched our bartender counting her tips before stuffing them into her ripped pocket. Once word had gotten out that we'd inherited our Dad's money, getting ass became as easy as taking a piss. Not that it was difficult before, but, overnight, the Steele brothers became the hottest thing to hit the South since sweet tea and Aquanet.

Yet again, Feen was right, but I didn't give a damn. Or maybe I just didn't want to hear it. Truth was, I'd never found a woman that truly challenged me. I'm a tough guy to challenge. I'm demanding, brash, self-centered, and impatient. Hell, I hate myself ninety percent of the time.

"You're just like Dad." Feen said, knocking me from my self-loathing. "He married Mom when she was sick. Took care of her until the day she died."

A lump caught my throat. Our Mom died when I was a toddler, but even then, my memories of her were so vivid that, at times, I felt like I could reach out and touch her. Hold her, ask her to take care of me. To change me.

I changed the subject.

"Anyway, I'm just saying... you could handle shit better if you tried to relax. Take some time off or something."

A moment ticked by. "Fine. I'll work on *relaxing,* as long as you suck less on the bottle—"

Just then... "I'd like to suck on that bottle."

I recognized the voice, because it sounded exactly like my own. Feen and I turned to see Ax striding through the bar, eyeing the headlining entertainment—Suzie's breasts. A witty comment to distract from the pain of the evening. It was in his eyes, it was in Feen's. And mine, too... before the whiskey kicked in, of course. I came to the bar to forget... and where one went, all went.

"Sorry I'm late."

"Work?"

"If by work you mean sitting outside Remy's cabin until the old bastard fell asleep, yeah. Work."

Remy Cotter, a retired Lieutenant Colonel with the Marines, was certain the ghosts of his Desert Storm days had jumped ship to the US to come back and kill him. Slit his throat, to be exact. So, he'd called us up one night and within six hours he'd lugged four boxes of canned sardines, three cases of Busch heavy, and three Ziplock bags of pills to the compound. Ten minutes later, we'd called in the local psychiatrist, Dr. Murray, who, to no one's surprise diagnosed Remy with a mild case of schizophrenia. The pills went down the can, and two new bottles were brought in. According to the doctor, Remy should be straightened out in a week. Axel caught the case, unaware that part of it would be providing a security blanket every night until Remy fell asleep.

Not all jobs were sexy Senator's daughters, celebrities, or presidential detail. We helped our own; always had.

"Where's Gunner?"

"He met with the family we just booked in. They're settled. He was in the shower when I left."

Gunner, a few years older than Ax and I, and second in line to the Steele throne, had taken the loss the hardest. Bought a new arsenal of guns, added an extra hour a day to his already two hour workout regimen, worked day and night to forget, and spent the remaining time at the range destroying targets, one after the other.

Ax, on the other hand, would randomly disappear for hours at a time, sometimes days at a time, into the woods. A jug of water, a few MREs, a can of Deet, a KA-BAR... and a look in his eyes that suggested he was about to wrestle a grizzly bear. My bet was on Ax—every single time.

We were all dealing with our Dad's death in different ways and I couldn't help but wonder when, or if, the grief would go away.

Ax looked around the crowded bar as Willie Nelson started singing about Pancho and Lefty. "Crowded tonight."

We glanced around at the laugher, empty pitchers, at the carefree cowboys and cowgirls, blowing off steam after a hard day's work. We watched as three ropes wound so tightly, each of us were about to pop.

Explode.

... And then I did.

As Feen and Ax started discussing work, I habitually tuned them out and decided it was as good a time as ever to take that piss I'd been fighting off since arriving. As I edged away from the stool, my gaze shifted to the trio of Stetsons, then to the quick, side glance Suzie flittered in my direction —a split-second before one of the rednecks reached forward and grabbed her goddamn tit.

'I saw red' is an expression I'd heard a few times—it doesn't fit. Not for me, anyway. For me it's more of a flash, a blind rage that takes over, blurring everyone and anything that comes between me and my target.

I lunged forward with tunnel vision as the world around me went silent. I grabbed the fucker's forearm, twisted with one hand, and with the other, slammed his face into the wooden bar. The *pop* of his nose breaking echoed off the walls.

His buddies didn't like that very much.

I did.

The next few seconds were like most bar fights I'd been

in—instant chaos. Good thing I thrived in chaos. The rednecks jumped up, sending their drinks on the floor and their barstools flying backward into the screams that had erupted through the bar. The biggest one locked eyes on me. A grin crossed my face as I released the titty grabber, once consumed with Suzie's nipple, now consumed with the blood pouring out of his nose.

I felt that tingle in my balls, that rush of excitement that I so badly craved every day. Just didn't expect to find it in the form of a few drunk cowboys. Regardless, there we were, and I was so fucking ready.

I missed a swing by a mere inch, and barreled into him. We caught the corner of a table, flipping it, along with its drinks, onto us. The table pinned my right side, allowing the cowboy to send a decent elbow into my ribs. Yowza. The blow of pain sent my adrenaline through the roof and I answered back with an uppercut to the jaw. We wrestled out from under the table—guy started clawing my skin like a damn girl. That pissed me off. He had a solid grip on my T-shirt, so I finagled myself out of that bear trap—God forbid he went for the leather jacket—and jumped to my feet.

I waited.

I waited for him to stand up to fight me like a man.

Kicking a man when he was down was for pussies, and if there was one thing the Steele brothers weren't, it's pussies.

Cowboy Joe jumped up, blood streaming out of his mouth from where I assumed I knocked out a tooth. I decided that new look would fit nicely with the can of Skoal in his back pocket.

Someone bumped into me once, and again, and I realized all hell had broken loose in the bar. A good ol' southern bar fight. Hell of a way to cap off the night.

Cowboy lunged forward, and tried another swing. I ducked, and connected my cheekbone with his knee.

Ouch.

Fucker got me with a punch, then barreled into me with the force of a Mack truck. His arm wrapped around my neck and he attempted to pull me down to the ground where he felt like he had the advantage. Well, the floor was sticky—with God knew what—and then there's my new jacket, so I decided at that moment that this thing was over.

As he reared back to try for another blow, I sent my forehead into the center of his nose.

The cowboy locked up like a plank and hit the ground.

K—fucking—O.

As I watched my unworthy opponent's head bounce off the hardwood floor, the chaos around me started to register. About that time, a body flew past me, followed by Feen, who lunged into his opponent, who might as well have been a rag doll at that point, and continued his fistfight with the other cowboy. And Ax? He had the other one, Mr. Titty Grabber, straddled on the ground, pounding him over and over, reminding him never, ever to touch another woman without her blessing again.

I was pretty sure no one in that bar would forget that lesson for a long while.

Just then—

Click.

I froze as the all-too-familiar sound registered through the screams and shouts. No one else heard it, hell, no one else saw it. I did. I heard it, because I was trained to. I was very, very familiar with the sound of a bullet sliding into a chamber. I was also very aware that it was two inches from the back of my head.

I raised my hands and turned around, and stared into

the barrel of a Smith & Wesson. Now, I'm a secure enough man to admit it—my balls might've leapt into my throat. It wasn't my first time with a gun in my face, but a first by a tweaked out drug runner who'd decided to show his buddies who was boss. Drugs took good ol' fistfights to a whole new level. It was a totally different fight.

Pupils dilated to the size of saucers, the tweaker incessantly licked his lips as his finger tightened around the trigger.

Shit.

I shifted to the balls of my feet ready to attack.

Turned out, I didn't need to.

Gunner, hair still sopping wet from his shower, flew through the air like a leopard attacking its prey, barreling into the tweaker. The two tumbled to the ground as the gun flew into the air. I caught it by the hilt.

The bar was quiet then, so eerily silent you could hear a pin drop—guns tended to have that effect on people. Everyone was on the ground... everyone except for four former Marines.

I felt my brothers step behind me, felt the brick wall of intimidation, adrenaline, and sheer terror they brought at my back. Eyes turned to us, wide, scared. Shocked.

I walked up to my brother, who'd just saved my life, and to the redneck who was about to take it.

Moments before Gunner choked the tweaker out cold, I bent down with a grin the size of Texas, and whispered, "Nobody fucks with the Steele brothers."

3

GAGE

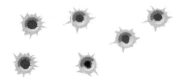

$\mathcal{T}$he cool, crisp air whipped around me, mixed with dust and dried leaves as I barreled down the dirt road on my Harley. My leather jacket flapped at my sides as I glanced at the line of motorcycles behind me, the dust storm twirling under the full moon then fading into the dark mountains that surrounded us. Feen, then Ax, then Gunner, each on their blacked-out bikes. Each still buzzing from the bar fight—and from the three free shots after, courtesy of Suzie—and each ready to get the hell home and call it a night.

The tilt of the moon reminded me it wasn't even midnight yet, and I began counting how many more drinks I'd need to fall asleep. Which, to my surprise, was followed by a pang of guilt as Feen's words echoed through my head.

"Less booze, Gage."

I cranked the music—good ol' classic rock—in an attempt to numb my thoughts. I wanted to forget, not worry about anything else. Not that night.

I inhaled deeply, trying to calm my racing thoughts.

It was fall in the Ozark Mountains. Even under the dim

glow of the moon, vivid reds, yellows, and oranges stood out against the dark mountains. It was my favorite season, hands down. Nature was as part of my family as our beating hearts. Ice, wind, rain, or scorching heat, we were out in it. Loving every second of it. But this season was different.

Very different.

It was one year to the day we'd received the call that Dad had died of a massive heart attack on his way into work.

That afternoon my brothers and I were on the first flights home.

It felt like yesterday.

God, I wanted to forget.

I took another deep breath and shook my head, willing the memories, the conspiracy theories, the flashbacks to dissipate as the compound—our compound—came into view. A three-story, eight-thousand square-foot log cabin mansion nestled between soaring oak and pine trees atop one of the tallest mountains in the area, sparkling with lights. Steele Shadows Security was founded by our Dad, six years before he died. A retirement plan, he called it. Something to do once he retired from the NSA—the National Security Agency. Our father, Duke Steele, proudly served his country, in the form of working fifteen hour days his entire life. It had paid off. He'd worked his way up, all the way to executive director of the organization.

Duke was a no-bullshit, tell-it-like-it-is kind of leader. He got the job done. Always had.

He was a good man. A better father.

As I climbed the paved driveway lined with antique lampposts, I gazed at the massive structure at the top of the hill. The crown jewel of the compound, as we'd begun calling it shortly after we inherited it, that was comprised of the main house which included a gym, basketball court, indoor and outdoor pool, a theater room, and three eleva-tors. Speckled around the house were an outdoor shooting range, indoor shooting range, an athletic complex with boxing rings, a handful of storage facilities, horse stables, and perhaps most importantly, three cabins to house clients who needed extra protection. Dad came from money—a lot of money—then amassed a fortune himself throughout his career. It wasn't until after he died that I realized how much money we had. The kicker of it was that I'd give every penny —every fucking penny—just to spend another day with him.

But, we couldn't. We had to get used to that.

Like a schoolhouse for wayward boys, my brothers and I lived in the main house, each with our own wing. Why? Because none of us had families of our own to take care of. Because our stepmom needed us.

Why? Because we all needed each other.

Then, anyway.

I parked in my designated stall of our six-car garage, as the boys rolled in beside me like roaring thunder through the night. A little rough around the edges with a few swollen eyes and busted lips, we walked into the house to the low melody of a piano. A haunting tune the color of black smoke.

"Dammit," shaking his head, Feen muttered under his breath.

"How was she when you left?" I asked.

"Fine."

"Fine, as in...?"

"Fine as in sitting on the deck with a bottle of wine."

"Did you actually go outside and check on her?" Unable to hide my accusatory tone, I yanked a beer from the fridge.

"No." He narrowed his eyes and looked me over. "Just like you didn't, either."

"Grab me a Shiner, will ya?" Ax nodded to the fridge. I tossed one to him as he continued, "She was crying."

"Crying?"

"Yes, the shedding of tears in response to an emotional state."

We wrinkled our noses as if the thought was so foreign we couldn't bare it.

"How do you know this?"

"Box of tissues next to the wine. Here." Ax tossed his beer to Gunner, then I tossed him another.

We popped the tops and sipped as we gazed out of the rounded kitchen doorway into the main entryway, deciding how to best approach an emotional woman grieving over the death of her husband. I, well, *all* of my brothers for that matter, prided ourselves for being able to tackle any situation. A crying woman? No way. We were known around town as four bull-headed, callous, cold-hearted sons of bitches. I'm assuming spoiled would be thrown in there too, if whoever said it didn't mind their teeth getting knocked out. We were known as American mercenaries. Trained to never show emotions, suck it up, and move on. We took care of our own by agreeing to sacrifice our lives to save theirs. Not by stroking their hair and listening to them cry it out. No we were stone cold, by all counts. Not here-you-can-cry-on-my-shoulder, let-me-help-you-through-it, would-you-like-a-tissue kind of guys. I knew women. Hell yeah, I knew women. Just not how to handle the enigma that was their crazy rollercoaster of emotions.

Especially once a month.

Christ.

There we were, standing in the kitchen like a bunch of

numb nuts trying to figure out how to console Dallas Steele, or perhaps willing someone else to do it.

Reading my thoughts, Ax cocked his head. "Where's Celeste?"

Gunner nodded enthusiastically—*Yeah, let her handle this shit.*

I shrugged. "Don't know. Been here as long as you have."

Ax rolled his eyes and swigged his beer.

Well, *fuck.*

"Come on guys." Maybe it was the kick in the ass from Feen earlier, but I led the way into the entryway where in the far corner, under the shade of the grand double staircase sat Dallas, eyes closed, fingertips flying over keys as white as the silk house dress that covered her pale skin. As if sensing us, her blue eyes drifted open, rimmed red above dark circles. Her long blonde hair was pulled back into a messy ponytail, with loose strands falling over her slender shoulders. Dallas Steele was forty-seven years old but looked half her age. A timeless, stunning beauty. That wasn't why Dad had fallen in love with her. Dallas was a child prodigy, a classically trained pianist by the age of twelve, and a talented painter, who graduated from Harvard with a double degree in computer science and politics. That wasn't what sealed the deal for Dad, either. It was her ability to hit a bullseye fifty yards away that did him in. Well, that and the fact that the woman had almost as much money as he did, and he didn't have to worry about her taking his. Dallas was a confident southern woman who never left the house without her nails painted and hair curled. She was a pistol, and had been as good of a stand-in for a mom that anyone could ask for.

Her eyes met mine and the house went silent.

A frown pulled her face—as much as it could around the Botox, anyway.

"What the hell happened to you guys?" Add intuitive to the list. Dallas pushed away from the piano and crossed the foyer, her eyes fading from grief to concern.

At least, I thought that's what that was.

Ax tipped up his beer. "Gage here can't handle his women."

"*Gage here* can't handle a man disrespecting any woman." I corrected him.

"What happened?" She crossed her arms over her chest, her tone sharp as usual.

"Guy got a little too touchy with the bartender."

Dallas's perfectly sculpted eyebrow cocked as she turned to Feen for verification. After a quick nod, she turned back to me.

"Good for you, then. Hope you taught him a lesson. Now, let's get some ice for that nasty baseball forming on your cheek."

"Nasty baseball? They have that on pay-per-view?"

She ignored my weak attempt at a quip and scanned the rest of her stepsons with an assessing eye. "All of you, follow me. Now."

We fell in line, as most did when Dallas demanded anything, and made our way back into the kitchen. After retrieving ice packs, antibiotic cream, and bandages she knew we'd throw away the moment she left the room, Dallas slapped a bottle of whiskey on the kitchen table and began tending our wounds.

"Aside from the fight, how are you boys doing?"

Boys—our titles since she'd married Dad. I sank into a chair.

Her question was met with silence, which was met with slitted eyes and pursed lips.

"I know you boys don't talk about your feelings but..." she blew out an exasperated breath. "We're all we've got now, and I want you to know that you can talk about things. *Anything.* You lost your dad, I lost my husband. We're in this together. Shit happens, life happens, and we make it through, and—"

"Except shit didn't happen, Dallas." Feen's voice cut her words like a knife.

"Feen, come on..." Ax muttered in desperation to stop the onslaught of conspiracy theories that was surely to follow. It was not the time. Hell, it never was.

"Come on, what?" Feen snapped back. "Come on and accept the fact that dad was murdered?"

"Jesus, Phoenix." I stood, recognizing the pitch, the heat of the words, spiced up by the three farewell shots we'd had at Frank's.

"Let him speak." Dallas demanded.

"Everyone in this room knows Dad didn't die of a heart attack." Feen glowered at each of us, daring us to challenge him.

I grabbed the whiskey bottle and chugged three good gulps, then handed it to Ax. He did the same, as did Gunner.

Feen continued, "Dad was murdered. Shit didn't *just happen.* Someone killed him."

In her ever-calm voice, Dallas responded coolly, "The medical examiner said it was clear that Duke died of a heart attack. There wasn't a question."

"Exactly!" Feen slammed his beer onto the counter with such force I was shocked the thing didn't shatter. *"Exactly.* There wasn't a *question.* No one asked a single goddamn question. There was no investigation, *nothing."*

My skin started crawling. I shifted my weight. We'd all thought the same thing and spoke about it on a few drunken nights. Other than that, tucked it under the rug with the rest of our feelings. The story, as we understood it, was that Dad suffered a heart attack, drove off a steep cliff, rolled twelve times when his car caught fire. He was pulled from the wreckage by the trucker who was behind him, ten minutes later. Dad was burned so badly he was unrecognizable. The coroner noted smoke inhalation in his lungs which meant he didn't die instantly. The man suffered until he took his last breath.

For me, the cause of death made sense. Dad was diagnosed with atrial fibrillation ten years earlier. The day he was diagnosed, he changed his eating habits, changed his workout routine, and began an aggressive pharmaceutical treatment. The Steele will to live was strong. The guy seemed to be healthy as a horse, but it didn't take five minutes of research to learn that the condition often led to a heart attack. Feen was the only one who questioned it. Seriously questioned it, anyway. Why, I'd asked him after the funeral, and with eyes as cold as ice he turned to me and said, *"Dad was murdered. I know it in my gut."* Since that day, Feen never let it rest. He'd spoken with Dad's colleagues—who, based on the mood Feen would be in after he hung up the phone—never went well. It changed our oldest brother. Hardened him. A ghost on his heels, never letting him rest.

Feen was not the man I knew. The brother I grew up with. He was tortured, tormented, conspiracy theories eating him from the inside out.

It was only getting worse.

Never one to back down to one of Phoenix's fits, Dallas stepped forward. "You need to let this go, Feen. I'm *telling* you; hear me. Let it go. It's been a year. It's not healthy for you, for your brothers, for your family. You need to let it go."

I focused on Feen like a kid about to be pummeled by his dad. Didn't want to be unprepared for the wrath that was about to be laid down. You see, with Feen, you always had to be on your toes.

Instead though, Feen looked at all of us, one by one, then said, "You're right. It's time to let it go." I didn't believe him. The disingenuous dismissal was interrupted by a chorus of bells and whistles.

Beep, beep, beep.

We all reached for our phones, alit with an alert.

Security breach, north lawn, point 1734.

I looked at Ax. "Any chance Remy is sleep walking?"

"I checked on him before I left for Frank's. He's knocked out cold."

"Let's check the camera." Dallas grabbed the iPad from the counter and began clicking through programs, entering security codes. "You said point 1734, right?"

Nods around the room.

After a few clicks, she turned the screen toward us, showing the heat signature of someone slinking from tree to tree at the base of the mountain.

Gunner and Feen reached for their guns.

I grabbed my own. "Well then, let's go see who our mystery guest is."

NIKI

*M*y feet had gone numb sometime after climbing out of the ravine I'd tumbled down, losing my one remaining shoe. More clouds had crept in, a sporadic thick blanket covering the only light I'd had—the only hope I'd had—reminding me I was no match for the environment I'd thrown myself into.

Correction—*been thrown into.*

I'd never seen such darkness as when the clouds greedily absorbed the moonlight. I'd stop, let my vision adjust to the inky black, allowing my other senses to kick into play, to smell and listen to the woods around me. Not silent, no, a thriving ecosystem of nocturnal creatures sneaking around, looking for their next meal. The breeze had picked up, chilling me to the bone and rustling the leaves around me, a white noise as unnerving as the fact that I was lost in the middle of the wilderness with no phone, no sense of direction, no food, water, no protection.

No light.

No, I'd never seen such darkness.

I'd never felt such darkness.

I had no clue what time it was. No clue *where* I was.

The only thing I was certain of was that the skinny bastard who'd been chasing me had given up a good hour earlier.

Where had he gone? Back to his truck? Back to hell where he belonged?

It was funny, I'd kept thinking about the things I'd left behind in my Jeep, wondering if the bastard had taken them... as if that was what mattered at that moment. But it did, to me. It was as if the violations kept coming. My body, my things. My new phone, along with my entire personal life inside of it. What could he learn from that information if he were to get past the security code? More disturbing, what could he do with it? The brand-spanking-new Louis Vuitton I'd gotten not two months earlier. The damn purse that made me smile every time I looped it over my shoulder. The purse that, to me, was a symbol of my hard work and independence... a stupid material thing, but those were exactly the types of things I didn't have growing up. To me, that purse meant something so much more than money. And he'd taken that, too. He'd probably sell it for twenty bucks... no... he'd trade it for a blow job at some hole-in-the-wall titty bar. The thought made me sick.

I wondered who, if anyone, had sent me a casual text not knowing that my life had been turned upside down, not knowing that I was lost in the middle of nowhere.

I'd stopped running, and had begun hiking, no longer focused on being hunted by a human, instead, focused on what animal might be hunting me.

I'd grown up in the woods—*in the sticks* was probably a more fitting description—and I knew what kinds of animals lurked in the miles and miles of dense forests that surrounded Berry Springs. Bears, coyotes, mountain lions, not to mention the snakes and spiders the size of your fist. Tourism was a huge part of the economy, but no one ventured that deep into the woods without a guide. Jagged cliffs, bluffs, and deep caves covered the area. Steep ravines that snuck up on you out of the blue.

It was dangerous. Especially for the unprepared.

I didn't do unprepared well.

I kept expecting to stumble upon a clearing, a farmhouse perhaps, that would lead me to a road that I could skirt along until I found some sort of civilization. Nope. It had been hours of aimless wandering through a vast mountain range where I wasn't at the top of the food chain. At one point, I'd heard the low rumble of a growl behind me and I was sure that was it. The drunk bastards who tried to rape and kill me didn't take my life, but in an ironic twist, an elusive black bear would finish the deed for them. Take what was left of me.

No doubt, an unfulfilling meal.

I was hungry, dizzy, and with each passing minute new aches and pains gripped onto me like an unrelenting force hellbent to take the last bit of energy I had. Hellbent on making me succumb to the evening, label myself a victim, just lay down and let nature take me.

Screw you, I said to that.

The swelling under my right eye had gotten worse. I knew this because I could see the bump in my peripheral vision. My shirt was barely hanging on, ripped from the attack, ripped from running through the woods. My stretchy yoga shorts, streaked with mud and water from falling more times than I could count. The last few times, I didn't even try to catch myself. I let my body tumble to the ground like a five-hundred pound weight.

Finding a place to sleep was not an option. Not only because my brain was still spinning with adrenaline—even though I was physically exhausted—and not because I knew that sitting still made me prime hunting bait for whatever carnivores slinked in the shadows, no, the reason I wasn't going to find a place to sleep was because it felt like giving up. Giving in.

I was not going to give up.

I pressed on, deeper and deeper into the mountains, with nothing but sheer determination driving me.

I'd been climbing upward, a fact marked by my burning quads, and I decided that was a good thing. Maybe if I got to the top of a mountain, I'd find a road, a house, something to guide me home.

Home.

A place that I knew would never be the same. The last time I was home, I was heading out the door to attend a yoga retreat at the luxurious Shadow Creek Resort. A weekend retreat to clear my mind, body and soul. Last time I was home, I'd stepped outside of my small cabin, inhaled the crisp, sixty-five-degree air and smiled, and thought to myself, *maybe I'll take the scenic ride home after yoga tonight.* Enjoy the beautiful evening. That small, simple decision had changed my life.

Last time I was home, I didn't know I was going to kill a man four hours later.

Over the course of my hike through the woods, I'd faced the gut-wrenching thought that I might lose my job. The job I'd worked so hard to get, the job I loved. The job I was good at. The job that was my life, my husband, kids, pets, everything all rolled into eight to five.

Fine, more like six to seven. I was a workaholic because I loved what I did.

Would they fire me?

The thought had made me gag.

My life had completely changed in the course of five minutes. What was ahead of me? I had no freaking idea. That scared the shit out of me.

The terrain became rockier, less trees, more dips and crevices promising to trip me with every step. I felt sick, sick in my body, in my mind. I kept climbing until finally —*finally*—I stepped into a small clearing marking the top of the mountain I'd spent the last hour pulling myself up.

My breath hitched as I spotted sparkling lights on top of the next mountain ahead of me. Lots of lights, a cluster marking some sort of massive building, then smaller groups of twinkling lights, perhaps smaller buildings, speckled among the thickly wooded trees. Below the structure, a row of single lights running vertically down the mountain as if a beacon lighting my way. I didn't think, didn't hesitate, and took off down the mountain with a rush of renewed energy. I knew nothing of the place I was going. I didn't care. It was my salvation. A means to an end to that horrific night.

A rocky valley marked the end of the mountain and the bottom of the next. The moon had decided to grace me with its presence, the beams swaying through the trees like silver waves. The mountain was steep, and going to be a hell of a trek. I noticed the underbrush appeared to be trimmed, the entire mountainside appeared to be landscaped. That confused me because there was no way whoever owned the castle at the top, owned the entire mountain... right?

Who had that kind of money?

If so, why out there in the middle of nowhere?

Well, I was about to find out.

My legs felt like lead weights as I took the first step upward, then the next. I'd officially crossed over to the manicured mountain when I froze, feeling a prickle of fear down the back of my neck. I don't know why, I don't know how I knew, but, at that moment, I had no doubt I was *not* alone.

My pulse quickened as my eyes darted around the moonlit dirt floor, willing myself to blend in with the surroundings. My senses piqued, focusing on the soft sound of the air through the trees, the stillness of night.

The stillness of whatever was stalking me.

An owl hooted in the distance, and like an alarm, ripped me out of fear and into action. I spun on my heel and took off, twigs and pine needles popping under my feet. Where was I going? I had no idea, but I was going to run. Even at that point of total exhaustion, I was not going to give into the nightmare of my day.

Out of nowhere, heavy footsteps ascended behind me, and I thought, he's finally caught me. This was it.

In an instant, the steps stopped, the air broke behind me followed by a *whoosh* of movement as my attacker's body slammed into mine with the force of a twenty foot wave. The air expelled from my lungs with a grunt. My legs gave out from under me as arms wrapped around my body and we tumbled to the ground, spinning, spinning, spinning through the underbrush. Groans and gasps escaped me with each rock I pummeled over.

Finally—*finally*—we stopped in an instant, on a dime it seemed, with my attacker straddling me. I knew immediately it wasn't my attacker from earlier. This one was bigger. Heavier. Much bigger.

My arms were pinned at the wrists above my head, my legs weighed down by his. My entire body was crushed. I looked into the eyes of the man who had me pinned to the ground, the full weight of his body against mine.

Moonlight slashed his face like silver warpaint, reflecting in piercing grey-blue eyes like the prelude to a storm that was about to unleash hell on everyone in its path. A storm that was either about to save me, or destroy whatever was left of me.

I was stunned, staring back into the only thing I could see of him—his eyes—my chest heaving, gasping for breath into a shadowed, stone-cold expressionless man who wasn't even breathing heavily. I'd think the guy was a statue if not for the warm breath escaping his lips. He was squinting, trying to see me through the darkness, as I was him. The wind shifted, the shadows reminding me of the masked men who attacked me. I struggled against him.

The grip around my wrists tightened. A bit more pressure and I was sure they'd pop.

"Let me go," I yelled against the silence. Then, using every ounce of energy left in me, I thrashed under him like a wild horse, bucking, writhing under his hold. *"Let me go!"* The panic seized me, the familiar rush of adrenaline shooting through my veins. "I'll kill you..." I said and meant it. "Let me *go.*" The words tumbled out along with my weak attempt to squirm my way out from under his grasp.

"Stop." The deep voice demanded, booming through the silent night.

And... to my surprise, I did.

I fell limp beneath him as he assessed me like a tiger about to attack its prey. Make it wait, make it a game, or go right for the jugular? I still couldn't see his full face. Still couldn't get a full read, and I knew he couldn't with me either. I decided that was to my advantage.

"Get off of me. I'll kill you..." My voice was embarrassingly weak and un-intimidating as I repeated the only threat that seemed equal to the moment. Hell, it was almost as if I'd said it like a question. Asking. *Can I even kill you?*

His eyebrow cocked and a small smile curved his lips, dispelling an ounce of my panic. Looking back, that was the first hint of the unabating attitude to come.

"Please do." His voice was smooth, deep, menacing, pinning me not only with his body but with his gaze now. "Put me out of my goddamn misery, sweetheart."

I blinked, the response throwing me off.

My wrists were released and although he was still straddling me, he raised up, his massive chest and shoulders evident through the black leather jacket he wore like a second skin. A dark silhouette looming over me like a king looking down on his servant.

He opened his arms widely, thick, swollen with muscles that only came from hours in the gym. He looked down at me, a black silhouette, his heart and vital organs opened up to me, his groin pressing against mine.

"Go for it." He said.

"Go for what?"

"Kill me."

My hands tingled as I flexed my aching fingers, my brain evaporating as I stared back. Any chance of putting together a quick plan of attack escaped with the rest of my thoughts. I kept my arms splayed out, like a whipped dog, too scared, or perhaps too smart to move.

A second slid by.

"Okay," he said. "Now that we've established that neither one of us is going to *kill* the other," he emphasized the word as if he was mocking me, "you're going to tell me what the hell you're doing on my land."

My land.

"I..." my voice was weak, shaky. I hated it. "I'm lost." I squeaked out like a terrified school girl. My gaze flickered to the outline of a gun on his hip, underneath the leather jacket.

"Are you alone?"

The question caught me off guard, another hint of things to come with this man. Who would I be lost with?

"Yes," I responded with a bit more control, and a touch of annoyance.

He shifted, his groin moving against mine in a way that had my body responding intimately—instinctively. He slowly stood, a massive tree unfolding itself against the night and pulled his gun from his belt. The moonlight caught him for a second, like a spotlight.

My stomach dropped to the ground.

"Get up."

My heart was a jackhammer, pounding so hard I could feel it in my throat. I mustered my energy, my confidence, my will to survive, and pushed myself off the ground.

And stood face-to-face with the most gorgeous man I'd ever seen in my life. My chin lifted—and a knot grabbed my throat. He was massive. A beast of a man that had to be multiple inches north of six foot. He had thick, brown mussed hair with sun kissed highlights at the top, sort of naturally untamed disheveled as if the guy hadn't seen a can of styling cream in his life, or simply didn't care. I assumed the latter. His eyes, dear God, a steely blue visible even through the darkness of the night. The color of a thunderstorm, a natural reflection of the man standing in front of me—strong, rigid, locked, chiseled jaw, radiating the power of a hurricane thinly concealed with whatever constraint this man allowed himself. I guessed not much. The thin T-shirt he wore fit snuggly against a chest I'd only seen in superhero movies. The badass leather jacket was the icing on the cake—as if this guy needed anything else to intimidate whoever crossed his path.

I should've been terrified.

… I wasn't.

No words were spoken as he lowered the gun, keeping his hand on the trigger. My eyes drifted over his face, somehow pulling me out of present time as if I'd been swept away from the darkness into some sort of quiet purgatory… *this* must be a mirage.

"What's your name?"

"Niki."

"Got a last name, Niki?" He slid the gun back into the holster on his belt.

"Avery."

Something flickered in his narrowed eyes. Did he know me? Did I know him?

"What are you doing out this far in the mountains?"

Killing a man.

I didn't answer, unsure how to launch into the last few hours of my life.

That made him impatient.

"Listen, there's about a hundred other things I'd rather be doing right now, and I'm not in the mood for games. I'm gonna ask you again, Niki, what are you doing out here in the mountains?"

"I was chased into the woods." I don't know why I didn't tell him that I'd been attacked. Perhaps because of the perceived weakness. Perhaps because of the embarrassment. Perhaps because I didn't want to reveal that much to a man who I knew nothing about.

"Chased into the woods by what?"

"A drunk bastard."

"Don't see any drunk bastards."

"You don't believe me."

"Of course I don't believe you."

"Well, that's just freaking great then." I stepped back, out of the shadows and into the moonlight, shook my head and laughed a humorless laugh. "Well, do you have a cell phone that I can use, at least? So I can call someone to tell my make believe fairytale to and they can come pick me up on a shiny white horse?"

The hard edges of his face faded as he looked me over—seeing me fully for the first time—from my shoeless feet, to my ripped shirt, and finally to the lump on my cheek. Something flared in his eyes.

"You've been hurt." He slowly stepped forward.

I'll never know why, never, ever, ever, but the moment the words left his lips, the heat of tears stung my eyes. A dam finally starting to break.

"Yes," I whispered, staring back, fighting the quiver in my voice.

You've been hurt.

The guy had no idea.

I blinked and clenched my jaw willing the emotions aside. Taking a deep breath, I jutted out my chin and squared my shoulders. *Do not fall apart,* I told myself. *Do not fall apart.*

His look shifted over my shoulder, scanned the woods, then back to me, and slowly trailed down my body, stopping at my feet. He reached for my hand.

I flinched, jerked it away.

His eyes widened for a split second at my reaction, then narrowed again. "Your feet hurt?" A sarcastic statement more than a question.

"They're fine."

"Really? Then we need to skip getting you back to your car and take you right to the podiatrist because that's the most wicked case of gout I've ever seen."

"What's gout?"

"I don't know. Something that swells your feet."

I looked down at the balloons that were once my feet, and the tiny sausages-for-toes that twenty-four hours ago had been pampered and painted a fire-engine red with little sparkles. Now, the skin matched the nail polish.

"Where are your shoes?"

I motioned behind me. "Somewhere out there."

"Okay then." He stepped forward and in one single motion, swept me off my feet, effortlessly, without so much of a grunt.

I wiggled against him. "What do you think you're doing?"

"Carrying you."

I pushed away from his chest. *"No.* I can walk."

"Listen," he snapped. "It's a steep climb up the mountain and your feet are ripped to shreds, and quite frankly, I'm tired."

"If you're tired, let me walk." He started up the mountain with a pace that had me both impressed, and clinging tightly around his neck.

"Not that kind of tired. Tired as in, I want nothing more than an ice-cold beer and a remote control."

I decided to shut my mouth and hang on for dear life as he navigated the mountainside, knowing every rock, dip, tree, it seemed.

Yes, it was his land.

We stepped out of the woods onto a narrow paved driveway that cut through the mountainside, snaking upward between lighted lampposts. I kept looking for a company sign. I knew it wasn't a hotel, because I knew all the hotels in the area.

My gaze froze on a dark silhouette beyond the tree line in the distance, then another beyond that. Two men, watching us from the shadows.

He didn't seem to notice, or care. My heartbeat started to pick up.

The driveway curved and the world opened up to the biggest home I'd ever seen. I questioned my sanity again, thinking it was another mirage, like a lush watering hole in the middle of the desert.

Like the man carrying me.

Landscape lighting illuminated a log cabin mansion with at least six peaks disappearing into the night sky, with walls of windows sparkling in the reflection of the lights. Massive natural stone pillars held up three floors of wrap-around porches and balconies. Trees closed in around it, making the shocking structure blend into the surroundings. Rock-walled landscaping ran through the yard, colorful mums decorating the steps that led to a rounded entryway with an iron chandelier hanging from its peak.

I twisted my head as we passed one of the men in the woods, his dark gaze looking at me like I was either a rabid raccoon about to attack, or perhaps, a raving lunatic who belonged in a padded room.

I looked up at the man carrying me, the chiseled jaw colored with a five o'clock shadow. The strong lines of his face marked with a steely focus.

We stepped onto the front lawn where the silhouettes finally emerged from the shadows, one by one, silent, stealthily coming into view. One, two, three men, as tall as trees, as wide as oxen assumed a circle around me, one in front, two in back, the man who found me, carrying me.

A small army, encircling their captive.

5

NIKI

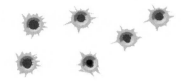

*T*hey led me up the steps, through the covered stone entryway with the iron chandelier, and finally, through the enormous double doors of the home.

I was met with the assaulting gaze of a blonde-haired stunning woman with eyes as cold as ice. The woman shifted her gaze to the man carrying me, and after some sort of nonverbal communication, she nodded and disappeared up the staircase.

"Kitchen," my guard dog demanded to his crew, and like a wave in an ocean, the men simultaneously turned and guided us across the foyer. I took a moment to look around the secret castle I'd found in the woods. Soaring ceilings with log support beams, sweeping windows with views of the mountains, bathed in the silver glow of the full moon. Stone floors speckled with furniture, colored like the nature outside.

It was like a tour inside *Architectural Digest*.

Strong. Masculine.

I was carried into a kitchen the size of my house, with stone floors, marble countertops, copper cookware, and state of the art appliances... and even one of those refrigerators that blended into the wall. I wouldn't have noticed it if not for the computer screen next to the hidden handle.

I was placed at a charming breakfast nook at the end of the room, next to windows framing a rolling front lawn speckled with lampposts. I stood, not sure why, and took a moment to look at the men flanking me like a prisoner. They weren't cagey, nervous-like, no, they were in ready-to-attack mode. I noticed they all looked similar, brothers no doubt about it, and each as ruggedly handsome as the one who hadn't left my side.

The room was so silent you could hear a pin drop, the tension so thick you could cut it with a knife.

They settled around me, two leaning against counter tops, one next to the doorway as if I was going to try to bolt, and mine, disappeared for a second, then returned with a first aid kit.

"Sit," he demanded.

My brows pulled together. I wasn't accustomed to taking orders from men, no matter the circumstance. He stared at me—they all did—as if I'd sprouted horns and wings. Apparently, they were not accustomed to anyone *not* taking their orders. I continued to stare back, hesitating in some sort of ridiculous pissing match, then realized my options were limited. Very limited. Whether I liked it or not, I was in need of help, and I was in their territory. It didn't take one minute to realize these guys were extremely territorial. So, I sat—as I was told—and assessed my current situation.

My Finder, as I called him in my head, grabbed a chair from the table, pulled it within an inch of my bloodied knee, kicked his leg over, and pretty much straddled me. He smelled woodsy, like country air, pine needles, with a hint of soap. All male. All sexy.

As he ripped the top off an antiseptic wipe, I glanced at the brothers, three pairs of eyes boring into me with the skepticism of a stray dog eyeing a piece of food. A rottweiler pit-bull mix.

"What's your name?"

My gaze shifted back to My Finder. "I already told you."

"Tell me again." Those grey-blue eyes flittered to mine, sending a flutter in my stomach.

"Is this a test to see if I'm lying?"

He cut a glance to his brothers, then focused back to the bump below my eye. "Yep."

"Niki Avery." I flinched at the sting as he dabbed the wound. He didn't stop, didn't pause, just kept cleaning.

"What are you doing out here, Miss Avery?"

"Niki."

"Niki."

"I told you, I'm lost."

"How long have you been lost?"

Since I was thrown to the ground and mounted like a piece of trash.

"Since I was attacked." My eyes drifted to the floor, shame heating my cheeks. I ground my teeth and looked up again.

My Finder froze, frowned, then pulled back, recoiling like a snake, a dark shadow sweeping over his face. Disgusted with me? Annoyed? The vein in his neck bulged. No, he was pissed, fuming as he stared back at me with a look that pinned me to the chair. Assessing, assessing, assessing, perhaps *seeing.*

If the room could've gotten any more silent, it did. A heavy, uncomfortable stillness as we gazed at each other. Him reading right through me. The hair on the back of my neck started to prickle so I glanced at the others, who were fixated on me with the same intensity. I then glanced at the clock on the wall, focusing on the *tick, tick, tick* while I grappled with the idea of jumping out the window behind me.

I couldn't take the silence, the metaphorical dress-down that these jacked-up dudes were giving me. God, they were high-strung. What were they thinking?

Did they know?

Know that I had been assaulted?

... Then, my question was answered.

My Finder leaned forward and said softly, "Tell me."

A lump formed in my throat. Yes, he saw. This stranger somehow knew exactly what had happened to me—whether he'd seen it many times before, I didn't know—but with that, came a comfort. A trusting.

A security blanket.

I released the breath I didn't realize I'd been holding and felt the damn tears start to creep up again. *Christ* I was a *mess.*

"Get her a drink," My Finder says to no one in particular, keeping his eyes on me. I couldn't tear mine away, either. My stomach was swirling, a tornado inside me as I stared back, pulling strength from the understanding of his gaze. Pulling strength from *him,* from this stranger who saved me from the woods.

A bottle of whiskey was set in the center of the table.

My Finder cuts a glance to his brother, this one almost identical to him. Twins.

"Water." *You idiot* was missing from the rest of his sentence. "And get a blanket, too."

The twin hurled a bottle of water across the room, and another delivered a blanket. My Finder wrapped the soft flannel around my shoulders, the warmth, the fresh scent of dryer sheets, shielding me, or perhaps hiding me from the mess I felt inside. He set the water bottle in front of me. I passed it by, grabbed the Johnnie Walker Blue and chugged until the burn down my throat began to distract from the emotions.

I set it down, the liquor like a shot of courage. After blinking the tears away, I cleared my throat. "What's *your* name?"

"Gage. Now that we got that out of the way, tell me what happened to you tonight."

I turned my head to the soldiers around me, but the man I now knew as Gage, placed the tip of his finger on my chin. He turned my face back to him. "Here." He pointed to his face. "Tell me right here." He leaned forward on his elbows, making me feel like I was the only person in the room.

I nodded, dissolving under his magnetic gaze, and launched into the attack that I knew had already changed my life. He listened, expressionless, unmoving, except for the slow clenching of his fists on his knees.

By the time I'd finished I swear to God even the ticking clock had silenced. I'd managed to fight the tears, thanks to the unrelenting rage that had surfaced while describing the attack. If they were surprised that I'd killed a man, they didn't show it. Then again, I doubted any of these guys allowed a pesky little thing like emotions to get in the way of anything. I felt like I was sitting buck naked in the middle of Times Square. My confidence, my armor, completely stripped of me.

I'd heard plenty of victims speak about their embarrassment after an attack. The notion always puzzled me.

Not anymore.

Sitting there, in the castle kitchen, I felt the most vulnerable I'd ever felt in my entire life.

Finally, Gage spoke. "You're sure two men? Only two?"

"Yes. Without question."

"You're sure the other one quit chasing you?"

"Yes, I'm positive. He meant to kill me. But I got away."

Gage turned to his brothers. "Get Jagg over here. And call BSPD."

The statues moved, one pulling keys from his pocket, another his cell, and the third, pulled his gun as he stepped forward.

"Gage," the tallest said, I guessed he was pushing forty. I concluded he was the oldest brother, based on the fine lines forming around his eyes, and the overly-protective demeanor. He nodded Gage over to the corner.

Gage squeezed my knee. "I'll be right back."

Although I couldn't make out most of what they were saying, two words cut through the silence as clear as a bell.

"She's yours."

6

GAGE

"*She's yours,*" Feen told me, the words laced with a warning as subtle as a train crash. As he disappeared out the back door, I looked back at our newest client —*apparently*—as she stared out the window pretending not to eavesdrop.

She was an absolute mess.

A devastatingly stunning, beautiful disaster of a woman.

Her arms and legs were covered with scratches and the beginning of bruising that was going to resemble a bushel of grapes. Her hand sliced from wrestling the knife away from her attacker. But all that was nothing compared to the shiner below her eye. A knock like that would give her a black eye for days, maybe weeks, and very likely be swollen shut in the morning.

Like her attacker's face when I got a hold of the son of a bitch. It didn't occur to me at first, no, like the blunt instrument I was, attack meant attack, simple as that. It wasn't until I'd gotten her inside, close to her, that I saw it in her eyes.

The pain. The *real* attack.

The survival.

Those fucking eyes, a doe-eyed deep brown, smooth, chocolate, as alluring as a nymph calling me to my death, and as paralyzing as the warning mixed with it. They were lined with a feather of long lashes sure to drop any man to his knees.

The eyes that had ignited a fire inside me so intense, I'd had to hold myself back. Hold myself back from grabbing every weapon I owned and hunting the son of a bitch down at that moment. Hold myself back from wrapping her up in my arms and carrying her to my bed.

She had long, brown hair that reminded me of silky caramel, with golden highlights shimmering like pixie dust under the harsh florescent light of the kitchen. And those lips, the lips she kept running her tongue over, pink and plump as a ripe strawberry. She was a handful of years younger than I was. Late twenties, early thirties? And that body—holy shit. One would think she'd be self-conscious in the skin-tight tank top and little shorts that hugged curves so dangerous they needed their own caution sign. Nope—maybe it was the blood that speckled them, the rips along the sides, but she didn't give a second thought to the racy attire.

Mess, disaster, whatever, this woman sparked something in me that I hadn't felt since I'd been knee-deep in a war zone.

It was immediate. Visceral.

Jarring.

The woman looked like a walking punching bag. But did she cry? Tremble in fear? Cower down to us when we demanded her into the house? No. Instead, she was controlled. Capable. Strong. In the face of any woman's nightmare come true, the one spoke with the strength and confidence of a seasoned soldier.

Her gaze flickered to me, then shifted to her shoeless feet, before another quick glance. Nerves, most would probably assume, but I knew better. This was a woman who knew her current role, knew she was in the hands of strangers, knew we were her only hope at that moment.

Knew *I* was her only hope... because... well, because *she's mine* now.

What else did I know? Two things. Two things, without question.

I knew Niki Avery was the sexiest fucking woman I'd ever seen in my life, and the second thing? I knew I was going to kill the bastard that tried to kill her.

I felt a burst of anger as I crossed the kitchen, wanting nothing more than to scoop her up and put her in my pocket, or perhaps in my bed... which was the last thing I should've been thinking about. I knew that. I knew what my brother's warning meant. If I screwed up this case, or *screwed the case,* he'd put me on probation, most likely in a caged facility promising ninety days to salvation.

Screw *that.*

Ax walked back into the kitchen, sliding his phone into his pocket. "Jagg's working a case. Says he'll get back to us. I called BSPD. Lieutenant Colson and another officer will be here soon." He looked at Niki. "You up for some interviews?"

"Of course." Her back straightened. Her eyes sparked with a shot of energy. Hope.

"Good." He looked at me. "Gunner's on the four wheeler heading to her Jeep."

And the dead guy... he didn't say it but based on the shudder that flew over Niki's body, she got it.

"Feen's already in the woods, searching for tracks."

"We need to look for tracks on the road, too. Get a make on the vehicle."

"I told you already," she snapped. "It was an old, red Chevy."

"I heard you," I said, the spunk of her attitude sending a tingle through my balls. She didn't appear to be intimidated by us, by me, and I wasn't quite sure what to make of that. "If we can get a good tread track, we can determine the exact model, maybe even the type of tire which gives the police a few different leads to chase."

"Will you pull my Jeep out? My phone, purse, everything's still in there. Hopefully, anyway."

"We'll take care of it. But not before the police have done whatever they need to do."

She nodded, then looked back and forth between me and Ax. I expected the usual "are you twins" question, instead I got—

"What is this place?"

"Steele Shadows Security."

Her beautiful dark eyes rounded. "You're *kidding.*"

"Nope." I wasn't sure whether to be complimented or wary.

"I've heard of you guys, or your company, anyway. You have offices all over the country. You do presidential detail, don't you?"

"We provide personal security to anyone who needs it. Twenty-four hours, seven days a week."

Her gaze scanned my body from head to toe, sending a squeeze between my legs.

"You're former military, aren't you?"

"You're observant, aren't you?"

She snorted and looked down. "I used to think so."

"Hey," Ax and I both said simultaneously, a talent we'd had since breath one.

"You did *not* cause this." My jaw clenched with frustration. One of the biggest hurdles we faced with sexual assault or domestic abuse cases was the victim blaming herself, or himself, for that matter. Although my immediate reaction was to slap some sense into the client, the training that our Dad forced us to take when he started the company—emotional intelligence or some shit—had me biting my tongue, and Ax, too.

She looked up and watched us closely, waiting for that pep talk we were supposed to be providing.

Well, she was in the wrong place for that.

I switched back to the original subject, and began to do what I did best. Lay out a plan of attack. "So, you came to the right place. First, you'll give your statement to BSPD, then we'll get your Jeep out once they release the scene…"

Ax's phone dinged. "Officer Haddix is here."

"The new guy?"

He nodded. "He's been with BSPD a few months now, I guess. Met him at Frank's a few times."

I glanced out the window, the night an inky black. "That was quick."

"Said he was a responding to a trespassing call."

My eyebrows raised. "Trespassing, huh? Where, exactly?"

"Old man Erickson's land."

I snorted. "That man reports trespassers once a week. Never caught a single soul on his land. Did Haddix see anyone?"

"Nope."

"See any vehicles?"

"Nope."

"Well, shit."

"Yep."

"Maybe Erickson has some security cameras we can look at."

"Nope. His security is his arsenal of sawed-off shotguns." A wicked grin crossed Ax's face. "Trust me, I've come face to face with that system a few times."

"I have no doubt you have, Bora."

"Bora?"

"The explorer."

"You mean Dora?"

"Yeah, you know, that cartoon chick."

"What does that have to do with me being on Erikson's land?"

"Because you disappear into the woods for days like a damn nomad, you idiot."

A quizzical looked crossed my brother's face. "... How the hell do you even know what Dora the Explorer is?"

An impatient exhale escaped my lips. "Am I the only one who watches television around here?"

"The pay-per-view." Ax grinned.

I glanced at Niki, whose eyebrow lifted.

"The fights." I grinned and shrugged, then turned back to Ax. "Anyway, Dora hikes and shit like that. You hike. It fit. Lay off me."

"At least I *remember* my hikes, and keep my pants up the whole time."

My grin deepened as I cut another glance at Niki, who was now officially avoiding eye contact.

Just then, a flash of headlights flashed along the walls. My hand instinctively reached for the SIG on my hip as I watched the black and white pull up the drive. It had been awhile since I'd seen the police outside our house. Ax disappeared to let Haddix in and I turned to Niki, who was focused on the car out front, not on me, the only one left in the kitchen.

"You ready?"

Her gaze shifted to me, a look of pure steel. "Yes." She said without hesitation, loud, strong, confident. My heart gave a kick.

My head turned to footsteps ringing over the stone floor, Ax's low, quick tone as he updated the officer on the mystery woman we'd found in the woods. I stepped a few inches behind Niki. I would have inched closer if not for the icy gaze I got from Feen as he passed by the window.

Officer Haddix strolled into the kitchen, a six-foot, solid two-hundred pounds of muscle and tanned skin. I'd never met him. The man was bald, all shined up like a cue ball, but he looked to be only in his mid-thirties which meant he either had pre-mature balding or took a page right out of the 'how to look like a beat cop' handbook. A walking stereotype, my guess was Haddix was teased in high school, and therefore, committed his life to getting drunk on authority and pulling over the 'popular kids' that had once teased him. In an ironic twist of fate, those popular kids were now nothing more than rotting bones of opioids. Yes, a walking stereotype... or hell, maybe the guy just liked the bench press.

He zeroed in on Niki, and I took a mental note of possessive rattle that flew over my bones. I wondered what the hell that was about. I hadn't felt possessive over a woman since... ever. I needed to cool it.

Remaining behind my client, I extended my hand and introduced myself. "Gage Steele, and this is Niki," I said as if I owned her.

His shake was quick with the aggressiveness of someone

who needed to prove something, and enough pressure to let me know he didn't care too much for me. A cop didn't like me? Fucking shocker.

"Lieutenant Colson is held up," he said. "He'll be out, but it'll be awhile. I already stopped by the scene." A glance to Niki confirmed it was as bad as she'd explained—most slit throats were—but he lingered, watching her closely for a second with a look I couldn't quite read. Then, he said, "I'd like to get started while everything is fresh in your mind."

"I'm ready when you are."

Heart, another kick.

Haddix nodded, then looked at me. "I'm going to need to ask you to step out."

"I'm going to need to ask you to remember who's house you're in."

"Listen, *Mr. Steele,* this is—"

"My house."

"Please, guys." Niki rolled her eyes. "Can we just get started?"

Haddix held my gaze for a second, doing his best intimidation stare, then yanked a notebook and pen from his pocket. Ignoring me now, he started the questioning with all the typical introductory questions—what's your name, birthday, the bullshit mandatory *get-to-know-you* questions. I noticed the guy watched her like a freaking hawk while she answered. It was as if he'd forgotten I was in the room. And I didn't like that. I listened closely to Niki's answers, too, although I already knew some it, and God help me, I wish to hell I hadn't.

Niki Avery had gone to Berry Springs school, as my brothers and I did. Despite the fact she was more than a few years younger than us, her life's story had made it all the way up to my grade. Niki grew up poor. I mean, food-stamp, hand-me-down-clothes poor. Rumor was she grew up in the middle of nowhere without running water or electricity. Electricity, okay, but no running water? The thought was as foreign to me as not having television. Or, Dora, for that matter. That was enough to earn plenty of bullying and gossip in a small town like Berry Springs, but no, that wasn't what sent her up the stratosphere. Niki Avery's fate as forever unpopular was sealed in stone the day her dear daddy went nuts. Rumor was, the guy started his mental break by pawning the only thing worth a dime in their house—her grandmother's wedding ring that had been passed down generations. Son of a bitch then met his long-time mistress—a part-time cashier at the discount grocery store—at a seedy hotel on the outskirts of town, skipped out on that bill, then blew every penny in his wallet at the casino bar. *Then* decided to mug the Oakwood sisters, two eighty-something-year-old church-going widows. He capped off that genius move with a stop at the liquor store where he stole a six-pack of PBR and got into a fist fight with the part-time help. He was caught an hour later, walking butt-ass-naked down County Road 2332, whistling the theme from Andy Griffith. It didn't stop there. Niki's dad lied his way through the interviews blaming the government, global warming, and a group of random teenagers for the shit-show that was his afternoon. That erratic behavior earned him a visit to the local psych ward, where he remained on psychiatric hold for forty-eight hours. After that, he was tossed in the county jail before packing up and leaving town—and his family—for good. 'Ol' Loony Avery' was the name he'd been given by the gossips. A nickname that didn't settle well with his daughter, apparently. A week after the incident, Niki Avery got into a fistfight with three of her classmates for making fun of her dad. Rumor was, she kicked their asses, making her a target for the rest of her school career. Niki's family was the laughing stock of the town for months. Her dad was a cheat, a liar, and a thief, and as I stared down at the back of Niki's head, I couldn't help but wonder if the apple hadn't fallen far from the tree. Maybe Niki was on a psychotic break like her dad had been.

I'd heard stories of women crying sexual assault when it simply wasn't true. They enjoyed the attention it brought them. Liked the pity, wore the title of victim proudly, as if it were a badge of honor.

Was that Niki Avery?

The enigma of the woman sitting in front of me was deepened even further when I learned that Niki held a bachelor's degree in Criminal Justice and Psychology, a masters in Legal Studies, and a law degree, and had recently accepted a job with a local law firm. She was only eight months into her career as a prosecuting attorney. *Holy shit.* Niki wasn't only hot, she was smart. And a freaking head doctor of all things. I inwardly laughed at this—she'd have a hell of a time analyzing my family, and me? Well, I'd have her running for the hills if she caught a glimpse of what went on in my head on a daily basis.

I learned she'd recently purchased her first home, a small cabin on Summit Mountain, and in an awkward back and forth, I learned that she didn't have any close friends. This surprised the hell out of me, but that was nothing compared to when I found out that Niki Avery was single.

I watched their back and forth, Haddix's laser gaze on her sending my instincts piquing. There was more to this interview than just the questions. Haddix was eyeing her with both skepticism and an edginess like he was expecting her to lunge forward and attack him at any moment.

Why?

Then, Haddix went in for the kill, asking her to retell the story of what got her lost in the woods in the first place. I listened to the story of the attack for the second time, my heartbeat increasing with each time her shoulders slumped and she forced them straight again. Every time she shuffled her feet under the table. My pulse was pounding by the time she explained the dirt in her hair. My fists clenched at my sides, the heat of raw fury climbing up my body like a poison. Her tone never wavered, her face expressionless as she told the story as if it had happened to someone else. Facts; she'd spit them out one after the other. No grey area, just *that is what happened, officer.*

I found myself inching closer to her. Why? No clue other than I wanted her to know I was there... and perhaps I wanted to remind Haddix I was there. Again, that possessiveness. *Of her.* This brought up a whole slew of emotions in me, a swirling mess taunting the professionalism I was supposed to have.

She finished her horrific story, cool, calm, and collected other than the incessant *tap, tap, tap* of her knee under the table.

A second of heavy silence slid by. Then, Haddix began his follow-up.

"Aside from the attendees at the yoga retreat, who knew you were going there tonight?"

"No one."

"You didn't mention it to any friends? Post on social media?"

"No."

"Do you recall anyone behind you as you drove to the resort?"

"Not that I noticed, no."

"How many men were at the retreat?"

"I couldn't give you an exact number. I'm sure the instructor could, but I'd say no more than ten, maybe less."

"Aside from the masks and dark clothing, what can you tell me about your attackers?"

"They were Caucasian. The bigger one was shorter than the skinnier one."

"How tall would you guess?"

"The skinny one... maybe a little taller than six feet."

"Tattoos? Piercings?"

"I couldn't tell."

"You're sure they were drunk?"

"I smelled liquor on one of the man's breath, yes."

"Did either of them say anything to you during the attack?"

"Aside from a few *fuck you bitch*'s when I fought back, no."

My brows lifted, along with the corner of my lip.

"And no," she cut off the officer before he could speak. "I didn't recognize the voice."

"Do you recall the size or type of the knife?"

"It had a black hilt, I remember that. It was a big, thick blade. Like a big hunting knife."

"Six inch blade? Eight?"

"Maybe eight."

"Smooth or serrated?"

"I don't know. I dropped it right after I..."

He nodded. "Miss Avery, did the two talk to each other during the attack?"

"To each other?"

"Right."

"I'm not sure. I don't think so."

"Did they both seem to be there willingly?"

"Willing? What do you mean?"

"Meaning, did it appear that they were both in on it together?"

"They were together when they ran me off the road. Got out together, so yeah, I'd say so."

"And to confirm, the man who threw you to the ground was—who you refer to as—the fat one?"

"That's right. The skinny one punched me initially, then the fat one pushed me to the ground."

"The fat one that you killed, correct?"

"That's right." Her voice cracked.

"And it didn't appear that one was forcing the other to participate in the attack?"

My eyebrows squeezed together, trying to figure out where the hell Haddix was going with this.

"No. I was the only one being forced to do anything," she said, attitude coloring her tone.

"What was the skinny one doing while the other had you on the ground?"

"Watching."

A moment ticked by.

Haddix leaned forward on his elbows.

"Miss Avery, does the name Ian Lee mean anything to you?"

Niki frowned. "No..."

"Never heard the name? Doesn't even ring a bell?"

"No. Why? Who is he?" Her face paled. She leaned forward. "Is that him? The man I..."

Haddix flickered me a glance. "According to the wallet in his pocket, yes."

"You know him?" I asked the officer.

Haddix nodded. "Everyone at the station does. Several DWI's, and one drunk and disorderly. Can't count how many times we've been called to his apartment for noise disturbances."

"Does he have a roommate?"

"Not that I recall. We'll check into all that."

I made a note of the name. "The second attacker has got to be one of his friends. Check his social media—"

"I wouldn't immediately draw that conclusion, but we'll check all angles."

"What do you mean, you wouldn't draw that conclusion?"

Fully annoyed with me now, Haddix dismissed my question. He picked up his phone and after a few taps turned the screen around to show a round-faced punk with a shaved head and neck tattoos. "Recognize him?" He asked Niki.

Her mouth dropped, looking into the face of the man she'd killed. "No..." she said, her tone breathless. "I've never seen him before in my life."

Haddix shoved the image closer to her face, his eyes boring into her. I wanted to slap the damn phone away.

"You have no past with this man? He's never wronged you, in any way?"

"No, I just said, I've never seen him before."

"No issues with him and any of your family members?"

"No. I have no connection to this man. Why do you keep asking?"

"Just trying to connect the dots." He finally pulled the phone away from her face. "To confirm, the top was off your Jeep this evening?" His eyes scanned her barely-there tank and tiny shorts.

"Yes."

He glanced at me as the same thought had crossed my mind. Misfit Ian Lee and his buddy on their way into town for more booze, sees a hot-ass woman in a low-cut tank top, alone in a vehicle in the middle of nowhere. Easy target. Done. A random act of sexual assault.

That ended up with one man dead.

Haddix closed his notebook and stood. "I'll speak with the bars in the area, and check security cameras if they've got any. We'll run the names of the yoga retreat attendees, as well as the guests of the hotel."

"And the truck?" Niki asked.

"Yes, we'll check with the DMV to see if anything matches the description along with your presumed height, race, and gender of the other attacker."

A lot to filter through was the undercurrent of his tone. But he wasn't done.

"Now..." He pulled a small camera from his pocket. "I need to get pictures of your wounds."

I shoved my hand on Niki's shoulder, squeezing. "Hang on just a minute. Don't you have a woman on staff that can come do it?"

"It's midnight. I can call, but it'll be awhile."

"No," Niki glowered over her shoulder with a look that'd make a normal man piss his pants. "Let's get it done. Now." She swatted my hand away, stood from the table, ignored me and addressed Haddix. "Where do you want me?"

"Here's fine."

I willed my legs to take a few steps back while staring at the officer, daring him to ask me to leave—half expecting Niki to, too. She didn't, and he didn't, so I stayed as he took pictures of her face, legs, arms, feet, tattered clothes, each *click* of the camera like a pop of a gun, inciting a firestorm of anger inside me. I fought the urge to rip the camera from his calloused hands and hurl it out the window. Haddix kept *looking at* her, watching her... not normally... like he was dissecting her. I didn't freaking like it. Niki turned her head to the side, jaw clenched, and revealed her stomach, cut and bruised. Then she turned around to display her lower back. My focus bore into her, wanting to tell her it was going to be okay. That she was being damn tough. But she avoided eye contact. More flashes, more restraint on my behalf.

As she lowered her waistband to show another round of scrapes, a small, red leaf fell to the floor. A flash of fire from a red maple tree in autumn. In the quickest movement I'd seen from her yet, she swooped down and picked up the leaf, carefully gripping it in her palm. A flicker of a glance to me, a flush on her cheeks.

What the hell was that about, I wondered. She held it tightly, guarding it from us, as a starving child would a piece of bread. The woman loved that leaf, or maybe just red maples, for whatever reason. Haddix glanced at me, and I shrugged.

Finally, Niki tugged down the top of her tank to reveal the beginning speckling of bruising above her left breast.

"That's enough," I snapped and stepped forward. Niki's quick side-eye prevented me from doing one of the dozen things I had rolling around in my head. Like pistol whipping Haddix with his own camera.

Headlights cut up the driveway.

"That'll be Colson," Haddix said casually as if he hadn't spent the last five minutes putting the final nail in the coffin of a woman who was already on the brink of an emotional breakdown. Then he paused, staring at her with that damn *look* for a moment before saying, "Just one more thing, Miss Avery."

Something in the officer's voice had my spine straightening.

"Just to confirm, you said you stabbed your main attacker in the neck, correct?"

"Yes," her tone ice-cold.

"Did you injure him anywhere else?"

"No."

"Not after?"

"Not after what?" She stiffened, her reaction now similar to mine.

"After you pierced his throat. You didn't injure him anywhere else?"

"No. I dropped the knife on the ground when he fell over. Maybe beforehand... maybe some scratches. I might have punched him. It was an *attack,* Officer Haddix, I was doing everything I could to get away. But after, no, I ran like hell."

"Where're you going with this Haddix?" I cut in, my patience cashed out.

The officer glanced at me, then back to Niki. "You're one-hundred percent sure you didn't attack him anywhere else with the knife? You're one-hundred percent sure you didn't have some sort of previous vendetta against Ian Lee?"

"What are you *talking* about?" Niki was out of patience, too. "Attack him somewhere else with the *knife?* No, I'm absolutely certain. And no, I've told you a hundred times, I *don't know the guy.*"

I didn't like him stressing Niki out more than she already was, plus, being ignored is one of my triggers—according to my brothers, anyway—so I stepped in front of Niki. "I repeat, Haddix, where are you going with this?"

"Yeah, why are you asking if I had a previous vendetta?" Niki followed up, elbowing her way beside me.

"Because, Miss Avery. Someone cut off Ian Lee's head."

7

GAGE

"*W*hat?" Niki squeaked, shock, horror, sliding over her face.

I put my hand on her shoulder. "What the hell do you mean someone *cut off* his head?"

"I mean," Haddix's gaze shifted between Niki and me. "Ian Lee has been decapitated."

"*What?*" Her voice pitched.

"Wait." I squeezed her shoulder, willing her to breathe, then addressed Haddix. "Where? At the scene?"

"I'm not going to make assumptions at this point, but his body is currently in the ditch in front of Miss Avery's Jeep."

"Without a head? Is that what you're saying?"

"That's right."

Niki's face matched the white of her tank top... the parts that weren't covered in blood.

"Just removed, or taken?" My mind reeled.

"Taken. The head is not at the scene, best I could tell from the little I searched on my way in. We'll look again, with more lights tonight and at sun up tomorrow."

"Hang on..." Niki raised her hand and shook her head,

trying to process that little—huge—development. "Someone cut off his head and *took it?*"

"Again, it's way too early for assumptions, Miss Avery."

"I didn't do that." Her eyes widened like a ghost's. "I didn't decapitate him. Why would—"

"Listen, *stop.*" I gave her shoulder another squeeze. "Breathe. It's fine if you did, regardless. Should've cut off his dick while you were at it."

"I *didn't* do it. I told you exactly what happened. *When* it happened."

The slamming of car doors outside broke the mounting tension.

Haddix looked out the window, then back at Niki. "Well, if you didn't do it, someone did. Unless the guy raised up from the dead and sawed off his own head."

Suddenly, Haddix's odd interview behavior and questions made sense. He'd assumed she'd done the grotesque deed, and maybe he still did.

"Is the knife still there?" I asked, hoping for prints on the hilt.

"Didn't see one." Haddix turned his attention back to Niki. "I'd like to take you back to the scene, to confirm that the body is exactly where you left it. But I'm sure Lieutenant Colson will have some follow up questions for you first. Please stay here, I'll be back in a bit."

Just then, the back door slammed, followed by a staccato of quick, heavy footsteps. Gunner and Phoenix. I watched Haddix disappear through the foyer as my brothers entered the room.

"Gage, a moment?"

Reluctant to leave Niki, I turned to her, blankly staring at me. I could almost hear the wheels grinding in her head. "I'm going to chat with my brothers real quick. You okay?" I had to fight to keep myself from grabbing her hand.

She nodded, dazed.

"Hey," I whispered.

Her dilated eyes focused on me, a fresh flush coloring her cheeks.

"I asked... you okay?"

"Yes," she whispered back, the nerves in her voice like a schoolgirl on her first day of kindergarten.

I ran a finger down her arm, unable to resist a touch, then followed Gunner and Feen to the far side of the kitchen. Niki had guided herself into a chair and was mindlessly twisting the unopened water bottle around in her hands.

My heart cracked. *"You always fall for the damsel in distress"*... Feen's words echoed in my head. A spike of insecurity gripped me. Maybe he was right, maybe I couldn't trust myself.

Maybe I needed to get a fucking grip.

I focused on my brothers.

"No trucks anywhere on the road, and no viable tracks." Gunner grabbed a towel from the dish rack.

Streaked with fresh dirt—a look that I realized I hadn't seen on him in a while—Feen slid his gun into his waistband. "There's a few tracks in the woods past the scene, definitely not solid or full prints. Broken twigs, leaves scattered; I can see the direction she ran. We'll head out at first light tomorrow and search."

"Guy's a mess. Well, what's left of him." Gunner shook his head. We'd all seen the horrors of evil, but not in our back yard.

"Wonder how long it took her to do that." My paranoid conspiracy theorist older brother said.

"She says she didn't do it."

"Oh, well then, if she *said*—"

"That's right, she said—"

Gunner held up a hand. "Fill us in, Gage," he said before a fight could ensue.

After sending Feen a glare, I did just that, reciting the black and white facts, doing my best to put a lid on the defensiveness creeping up.

"*Niki Avery.* You know who she is, right?" Running his fingers through his hair, Feen shook his head. A few specs of leaves fell to the ground.

"Yeah, I know who she is."

"Jesus *Christ.*" Gunner laughed, putting the pieces of the puzzle together. "'Ol Loony Avery's daughter. The town liar. You're fucking kidding me."

"What's that got to do with anything?"

"How can we believe a thing this girl is saying?"

I opened my mouth to expel the anger boiling up my body, but the thing was, how did I know Niki Avery wasn't full of shit? A nice face, perky tits, and a tight ass didn't mean the woman was incapable of a lie. Hell, in my experience, the more perfect the face, the deeper the lie. It was obvious that Haddix wasn't sold on her story, either.

Feen continued his rant, "She could be lying about everything. Maybe she and the guy who chased her were in it together. Hell, maybe she was partying it up with the losers and things got out of hand. Or maybe she wasn't even chased in the first place. This could be a setup to get into our compound."

"Give me a break, you paranoid—"

"That's *enough.*" Gunner snapped, losing his patience with us. Another minute, he was likely to knock us both out.

"I'm telling you, she says she didn't do it. Says she cut his throat and ran."

Feen flashed me that disapproving look that had a way of making me feel three inches tall. "You believe her?" He asked.

"I do." I squared my shoulders and bowed up, a familiar reaction to my older brother's consistent disappointment in me.

"She's a pretty face. That's it, Gage. Take your fucking blinders off."

"What the hell's that supposed to mean?"

"Enough." With his impeccable timing, Ax entered the room, commanding silence as he did when Feen and I were engaged in our usual tit for tat.

I took a deep breath, along with a step back, but couldn't bite my tongue. "Okay, I want to get one thing clear first. Are we all in agreement that regardless of what happened, this woman was attacked? Shit, she looks like a bruised peach."

Nods around the group.

"Okay then, so she was attacked, then let's assume she did decapitate the guy afterward—that she was *strong enough* to do it. That means you're thinking that she slit his throat, then what? She takes the time to cut off the rest of Ian's head? And where the hell is the other guy while this happens?"

"Could have done it with her." Ax said matter-of-factly. It made more sense than her doing it by herself.

"Fine. But why? What's the point?"

"Revenge for something. Or, like Feen said, something got out of hand. Or, hell, blind rage. Gage, how many times have we seen that? Guy's beating a man to death and continues to smash his face into his skull because of the rage. The adrenaline. The release that comes with beating and killing a man."

"No. You're crazy. No way."

Ax glanced at Niki, still sitting at the table, then back at me. "You don't know her, Gage. *We* don't know her. We don't know a thing about this chick. When people come to us for protection, we know their entire story, have read the police reports, the whole nine yards. This chick just showed up in our front yard. We don't know shit about her."

"We will soon." Feen looked at his phone. "Jagg's going to run a check on her."

My eyes rolled back into my head.

Ax cut me a *cool-it* look, then did what he does best, analyzed facts. "So two guys attack Niki, and she kills one, Ian Lee. Either at that point, or within a few hours later, someone cut off Ian's head and took it with them. Either she did it, the accomplice—skinny one—did it, or someone else who drove up on it later. Period. Let's start with scenario one. The chick—"

"Niki."

Feen snorted.

Ax continued, *"Niki* kills the guy, cuts off his head, and takes off with it—"

My gaze leveled his. "Niki does not have a human head hidden in those yoga shorts, Ax."

"Well, if anyone would know, it's you. Agreed, though, that this seems unlikely. Second scenario is that the second attacker went back and did it after he chased her through the woods."

"Why, though?" Gunner said. "We're assuming the two were buddies, right? Why would he cut off the guy's head?"

We all frowned at each other, trying to put the pieces of a puzzle together that was getting larger, and frankly, weirder by the minute. I never was a fan of puzzles, anyway. That was Ax.

"Okay, option three... someone else entirely did it. Solo, or a third accomplice."

"During a very small window of opportunity."

"Right, so, two hours or so."

"Niki said she didn't see or hear any other cars before they ran her off the road, or while she was in the woods. And no one lives down this road beside us, Ax. Who would be this deep in the mountains, late at night?"

"Old man Erickson. Remember, Lieutenant Colson said he'd called about trespassers..."

I shook my head. "His house is on the other side of the river, and the main bridge is down. Guy never leaves his house, and if there really were people on his land—there never are when he calls—they wouldn't have had time to do all this and leave without a trace. So, who else?"

Phoenix's gaze slid over my shoulder. "Our staff."

"Jesus *Christ,* Feen, you think one of our staff is involved?"

"Feen's right," Ax jumped in. "We need to consider all angles and look at everyone in the area. The timeframe is too short to not consider it. We live on miles of private, restricted property—our property. It has to be someone close. We need to pull the list of who's working tonight. If nothing else, maybe they saw something."

Gunner nodded.

A moment slid by. I raked my fingers through my hair, feeling the twinge of a headache between my temples. "But guys...why *take* the head?"

"We need to search the scene, the woods. See if whoever did it actually took it with them or dumped it somewhere."

Feen nodded, then started toward the back door. "I'm going to go talk with Colson."

"Me, too." Gunner grabbed his phone from the counter.

The back door slammed shut and Ax hung back. "I checked the security cameras on the north lawn. It was only Niki in the woods. No one else. That part of her story checks out, at least."

"She's not a liar," I mumbled as I looked over my shoulder at her.

My twin brother put his hands on my shoulders, demanding my attention on him. "I believe you, and I believe her. Just keep a clear head, alright?"

I took a second to wonder what, exactly, a clear head was.

"I'm going to check out the scene again."

"I'm going to stay with Niki."

"Figured as much."

8

NIKI

*M*y attempt to eavesdrop failed as Gage and his twin discussed something—about me—in the corner, their faces expressionless, voices monotone. I got the vibe I wasn't the only woman to be whispered about in their kitchen. I tucked my red leaf back into my waistband and wrapped my arms around myself. My stomach was in knots, swirling with the grotesque image of Ian Lee's decapitated body.

I glanced down and grimaced, my face squeezing with a rush of insecurity. My legs, arms, clothes, entire body was covered in dirt and mud, the grime suffocating my skin. I was an absolute, total train wreck. I was embarrassed. Not only because of how wretched I looked, because I was weak enough to get beaten up so badly. Screwed up, I know, but that's how I felt. No matter how much I tried to will the thought from my head, it remained like a stain, inter-grained into this new woman I'd never met before. I clenched my jaw, disgusted, and began scrubbing my arms.

What a total mind fuck.

A towel appeared on the table as if my thoughts had

been said out loud. Gage stood above me, his looming presence making me stop cold, a side-effect of this man that was quickly becoming habit.

He squatted down in front of me and reached for my leg. "We need to get you cleaned up."

I pulled away. "I can do it." For all the dignity I had left in me, *I can do it.*

His brow slowly lifted at my recoil, then he shrugged, flippant. "Alright, then. You need to start with the bottom of your feet. No telling how much bacteria and nasty shit you picked up running through the woods. Come on. Let's go. Now."

Before I could protest, I was swept out of the chair and into his arms, another act becoming habit.

This one I could handle.

I was whisked to the counter top, my dirt and blood-covered legs swung to the side and placed into a sparkling copper sink.

The water was turned on and I watched Gage while he waited for it to warm up. Silently. Patiently. Then, he pulled the nozzle and ran the warm water over my shins. A million needles pricked my skin as blood and mud swirled down the drain, beginning to wash away the nightmare that had been my night. If it could only wash away the memories, too. Reading my thoughts, he began to rub my legs, cleaning, careful to avoid even the smallest cut. A tingle rushed over my skin as I watched him, his big, rough hands cleaning me. He was gentle, a juxtaposition to the tough, rugged, beast of a man I'd met in the woods. His hands, along with his gaze, slowly swept upward to my knees. My pulse picked up.

Those stormy irises skimmed my body, slowly. Seductively, a thinly veiled hunger as intense as the beating of my heart.

His eyes met mine.

Butterflies tickled my stomach.

"Well, well, *well*... I'd say *'take it to your room'* but your bed is covered with beer cans."

Startled, I ripped my eyes away and felt a rush of embarrassment as I looked over my shoulder toward the gruff, female voice booming from the doorway. Her jet black hair was pulled into a messy bun on the top of her head. Sharp, piercing blue eyes against tanned skin and bright red lips. Colorful tattoos covered her toned arms, running underneath a faded, holey T-shirt that read *Bad Motha Fucka*. She wore tattered skinny jeans emphasizing a curvy, fit body, and flip flops. She was every sexy super-heroine... on steroids.

Gage didn't pull away as I did, no, instead he left his hands on my legs, continuing to caress in some erotic hot-nurse scenario, now a threesome. The heat rose from between my legs to my cheeks.

"Niki, this is Celeste Russo, former spec ops Marine, current receptionist and office manager of Steele Shadows."

Eyeing me like a stray dog, Celeste sauntered over, every inch of her letting me know that I was in her territory.

"This is the chick who got herself lost in our woods?" She asked Gage, ignoring me.

My brow cocked. I swatted Gage's hands away, then fired back. "That's right. I decided to get myself lost right after I dropped off that T-shirt at the second-hand store."

The black Raven's eyes popped, followed by an ear-to-ear grin. I didn't blink, unwilling to back down from the 'former spec ops Marine'.

With a gleam in her eye, she turned back to Gage. "Well, alrighty, then. If there's any more like this in the woods, maybe we can hire them to look after Remy."

Gage grinned.

Then, she looked at me, her expression softer. "Welcome, and..." Her face dropped to serious. "Nice aim." A quick nod, a nonverbal, you-did-what-you-had-to-do.

I nodded back, and decided that I liked this brick-balled badass. And also wondered how many men *she'd* killed.

"You'll have to excuse Celeste. She needs to work on her people skills."

"Good thing that isn't a very important quality for a receptionist."

This quip earned me chuckles from both.

Celeste shifted her attention to Gage, who had moved onto dabbing my feet with ointment before wrapping them up. "I just spoke with Jagg." She said. "He's not going to be able to come by tonight. Something about thirty pounds of cocaine and prostitutes' vaginas."

"Sounds like an interesting search and seize."

"Exactly. He wanted me to tell you he's sorry you couldn't make it."

Gage smirked and glanced at me. A ladies' man, then. Not that I was surprised.

"Anyway, he said he'll come by tomorrow. Everyone's down at the scene now." She turned to me and said matter-of-factly, "You're going to be okay. You're going to be taken care of. Anything you need, you let us know." She nodded to Gage. "Well, these bastards might not be too much help, but I can help you with anything... you know, girly things you might need."

"Gross," Gage muttered.

"Not everything girly is tampons and anti-itch cream, Gage."

"Anti-itch cream? Must be talking about Gage's latest date." A tall, beefed-up guy breezed into the kitchen, his dark, mussed hair curling out from under his baseball cap, his sun-kissed skin a flawless tan. He wore ripped jeans, a Steele Shadows hoodie, and ATAC boots. "You know, that one with the massive—" He stopped cold and zeroed in on me, my legs dangling in the kitchen sink.

"Whoops, sorry." An easy smile flashed across his face, perfect teeth and a bad boy twinkle in his eye that I had no doubt many women had fallen to their knees over. "I'm Wolf," he said. "Head of security. You must be our guest of the evening, Niki."

"News travels almost as fast as that report I asked you to get me." Gage's eyebrows raised.

"Sorry..." Wolf sauntered into the room with an ease that suggested—again—that I hadn't been the only woman to show up at the front door. Cop cars out front, bloody legs in the kitchen sink... just another day at the park for the guy they called Wolf.

"...the game, you know. Overtime." He yanked a beer from the fridge, his indifference to me oddly soothing at that moment. I liked him.

"Yeah, you owe me a thousand bucks, Wolf."

"You owe me a new truck, Gage."

"Call it even."

Wolf snorted, sipped, then flickered a glance at me before saying, "Hear we got a headless body on the road." He focused on me. "Ian Lee. Nice work."

"Wolf, come on, *sheesh...*" Shaking her head, Celeste gave me a grim look. "You'll have to excuse Wolf. He also needs to work on his people skills... and gambling apparently."

"I'm sorry, you're right." Wolf set down his beer and turned fully to me, tipping an imaginary hat and unfurling his hand as one would The Queen. "Miss Niki Avery, my name is Sir Wolfgang Blackwood," he said with an overly-emphasized English accent. "An unfortunate name given to me by my parents, who were both drunk at the time of my birth. While most men would shrink at the nicknames I've been called, I, Miss Avery embrace it, because, you see, in my pants lies a six-foot—"

"Oh my *God,* Wolf. *Enough.*" Celeste shooed him away from the counter.

Gage grinned and shook his head at this.

Laughing, Wolf stepped back. "Come on. Just trying to lighten the mood. Get this girl cleaned up, will ya?" Celeste and Gage rolled their eyes. He continued the one-man play, "By the way, Dallas is going to flip when she sees the trail of mud in the entryway. Who the hell came through the house? A pack of Clydesdales?"

Celeste frowned. "Yeah, I saw that. Why didn't you have everyone come in through the garage? You know how she gets."

"That'd be Haddix. Must've left it along with the trail of testosterone he's got coming out his pores."

"What'd he do? Spend his evening in a mud pit? Dallas is not gonna be happy; just sayin'." Wolf swigged his beer.

Gage shrugged. "Where you been, anyway?"

"In my office."

Celeste looked at me. "By office he means our command center, on the top level. We'll show it to you while you're here; pretty cool. Wolf lives in a small cabin just off the land but is *always* here."

"Don't pretend like you don't like it. And my *command center* will be much cooler as soon as your boy here approves the new cameras I want to get."

"Approved." Gage said. "Use the one-K you owe me. What's got you working so late tonight?"

Wolf glanced out the window for a moment before

saying, "Working on something for Feen."

"What?" Celeste frowned.

"Oh, you know Feen, always up to something."

I glanced at Gage, his eyebrows knitted together in concern.

"Guy needs a girlfriend," Celeste grumbled.

Wolf wiggled his eyebrows at me.

Gage's grip tightened on my knee, earning a cocked brow from Celeste.

"Alright," he said quickly, changing the subject. "Um, let's head down to the scene and see if they need anything."

I caught the side-eye from Celeste, and looked down. Gage's abrupt switch of conversation was as subtle as an earthquake, and Celeste didn't miss much.

Gage yanked a towel from below the sink and handed it to me. "I'll be back. Lieutenant Colson is going to want to interview you again. You up for that?"

"Yes, of course."

He shifted his attention to Celeste. "You two girls do whatever girly things you need to do."

"Itch-cream is in Gage's room next to the condoms and anal beads," Wolf needled.

"Ah, that reminds me, I meant to give those back to you," Gage grinned, then turned and strode across the room, Wolf on his heels.

Celeste called out after him. "Gage?"

"Yeah?" He responded, keeping his pace and without so much of a glance over his shoulder.

"She'll be in Cabin 1..."

He wagged his index finger in the air as he nodded, before disappearing around the corner.

I looked at Celeste.

What the hell was Cabin 1?

9

GAGE

"*I*'ll be outside in a minute."

Focused only on the text message he was sending, Wolf nodded and pushed out the back door. Frowning, I turned and followed the hushed voices coming from the staff kitchen—a small kitchen just past the main one. A ridiculous addition to the house, but one that Dad had said was necessary for resale value. Whatever.

It was past midnight at that point and all the insomniacs were down at the scene. Who was up for a late-night snack? More importantly, had they seen anything that could help piece together the evening's events? Or, as Feen would ask, did they *know* anything?

I paused at the doorway, straining to listen to what sounded like an argument. My mind raced putting together the list of staff we'd had working that day, followed by self-disgust when I couldn't name them all. Dad knew everyone by first and last name, and every detail of their immediate family. Feen did too, for that matter.

What the hell was wrong with me? When did I get so self-absorbed?

Repulsed at myself, I stepped out of the shadows and into the kitchen.

My eyebrows popped.

Wearing one of her usual paisley print muu-muu dresses, our head housekeeper, Opal Mallick, stood with her arms crossed over her voluptuous chest decorated in a dozen beaded necklaces, her grey dreadlocks pulled back at the sides with glittered ribbons. She also wore one hell of a pissed-off expression on her face. Her gaze immediately shifted to me, her eyes widening. In front of her stood none other than Remy Cotter, our retired naval client, wearing nothing but a stripped pair of pajamas and slippers. Following her gaze, Remy turned, his face flushed, his eyes hard.

"Mr. Steele," Opal quickly stepped back. "Can I get you something?"

Keeping my eyes locked on Remy, I crossed the small room. "Everything alright, Mr. Cotter?"

His gaze flickered to Opal. "Yes, just came out to see what all the commotion was about."

"Ax mentioned you'd fallen asleep hours ago."

"Well, I woke up. Heard car doors slammin' and came outside to make sure no one was lurking around my cabin."

"Mr. Cotter—"

"*Remy,* Gage, *shit,* I've told you a hundred times."

"*Remy,* sorry. Remy, Dr. Murray said it's best to stay inside until your medicine gets ironed out."

"Well maybe if you'd give me back the gun you confiscated from my bag when you booked me, I wouldn't feel like I needed to investigate noises outside my cabin."

I glanced at Opal, who'd slid her red-rimmed glasses to the tip of her nose, her eyes darting between the two of us.

"Let's get you something to drink, and I'll have Ax take you back to your cabin."

"I don't need Ax to take me anywhere, Gage."

"I know you don't, but Remy, as long as you're here, you'll mind our rules. No one on the ground after sundown without an escort. Understand?"

He grumbled something that involved me falling off a tall cliff.

I pulled my phone and texted Ax, then put my hand on Remy's shoulder. "Take a seat in the library, Remy. Opal will bring you some tea, and Ax'll be up in a second."

"Fine."

I waited until Remy disappeared into the library before turning back to Opal, who had already put water on to boil.

"What was that about?"

She shook her head, pulling a tea cup from the cupboard. "Grab a paper towel, will you? He was pestering me about getting his gun for him. Wants it in his cabin. Crazy old bat, he is."

"Well, he can't have his gun while he's here, and that's that." I ripped a paper towel from a hook just above a bubbling tub of water in the sink. "What're you bleaching in here?"

The tea cup slipped from her hands, shattering on the stone floor.

"Oh... *no.*" She shook her head and started to squat.

"No, Opal, I've got it." I swooped down and picked up the glass, eyeing her. "You okay?"

"Yeah... yes, sorry." She was flushed, embarrassed, perhaps. "Remy got me all worked up is all. Sorry." She glanced at the sink. "And I'm just doing the monthly deep clean of utensils. Sorry about the cup." She wrung her hands together, the dozens of gold bracelets clanking against the silence. Apparently, everyone was on edge, and that was a look I hadn't seen too many times on our head housekeeper.

Dad had hired Opal to help with the household not long after losing mom. They'd met on a street corner where Opal was selling paintings and psychic readings. For ten dollars, she'd tell you your fortune and sketch your profile. At sixty-one years old, Opal was a self-proclaimed hippie and ran the house, and the staff, with an iron fist and dry wit to match. I'd always liked her. Dallas, on the other hand, had not. It was rumored that Dallas didn't appreciate the fact that Opal lived in the basement, which had been renovated to her specifications—lots of windows, and lots of dark colors. A contrast that was Opal. A presence that Dallas didn't care for.

Opal grabbed one of the crystals dangling around her neck, worry squeezing her bushy eyebrows. "I was in my room and saw Remy coming up the back path on his golf cart. Coaxed him inside for some tea until I could wrangle you boys to deal with him... but it looked like you've had your hands full tonight." She poured boiling water into a new cup and dipped a tea bag. Steam swirled up from the edges, concern shined in her eyes. "What's going on with the cops out front, dear?"

"A little incident in the woods."

"A very pretty incident."

I glanced down.

"Well, I know you boys will take good care of her. I'll get this tea to Remy."

"Opal, do you know if anyone left the grounds tonight? Did you, by chance?"

She frowned. "I didn't. Was down at the stables for a

while before heading back to the basement. And no, I'm not sure about anyone else. I can ask around if you'd like?"

"Please, and would you mind sending me a list of everyone's schedule this week? Especially who worked today?"

"Of course."

"Thanks, Opal."

As I made my way out the kitchen, my gaze locked on the carving knife soaking in the sink.

10

NIKI

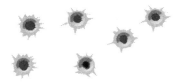

*T*wo hours of more interviews, and one horrifying trip back to the scene later, I was guided out the back door by Gage while his brothers and Celeste congregated in the kitchen for one last night cap.

The night had cooled, dipping into the fifties, a prequel to the winter to come. The seasons were changing.

Fitting; my life was changing.

Gage led me down a small pebble rock way, lined with decorative lights. Last I'd looked it was close to one in the morning. It felt like I'd been up for weeks.

A cloud drifted, the silver glow of the moon washing over the mountains in the distance. The night was still, haunting, as if all its creatures sensed the evil that had taken place hours earlier.

I was exhausted, mentally and physically, in pain, and compounding that volatile state was the fact that I'd agreed to stay overnight at the compound in the care of Steele Shadows Security. Gage, specifically, according to Celeste.

I had no choice, really. My Jeep had been confiscated, towed out and scheduled to be sent to a forensics lab first thing in the morning to be scanned for DNA or trace evidence. I had no phone to call whatever surface-level friends I had and ask for a ride and a place to stay, and even if I did, the thought of retelling the story one more time made my stomach sour.

Perhaps the most unnerving thought of all... was wondering if whoever tried to kill me was still looking for me?

A brief look through Ian Lee's social media didn't provide many clues, other than the fact that he was a socialist bigot who didn't believe in conformity. A grand total of six posts and only a handful of followers didn't amount to many leads to chase.

Ian Lee was a twenty-four year old Berry Springs native who worked construction, when he wasn't serving jail time for one of his many misdemeanors. I'd never seen the man before in my life, but when they'd pulled up his social media account, I'd almost thrown up on their company-issued shoes.

No matter what Ian had done to me, no matter what he'd planned to do to me, nothing seemed to justify the ending of the man's life who grinned into the camera holding a can of Budweiser.

A grin no more.

And I did that.

Then, someone else decapitated the guy.

Lieutenant Colson had promised to push a warrant for Ian's phone records, but that could take days. They'd promised to talk to his friends first thing in the morning, but considering most of them also had rap sheets, the odds of them opening up were slim to none.

As the night dragged on, it was obvious Officer Haddix considered my attack a random act of violence—one that happened all too often. But who the hell carved the guy after the fact? And, why? According to Lieutenant Colson, the man who chased me into the woods would possibly try to find me again. Kill me, was what he meant. The agreed assumption was that the guy was concerned that—considering I'd survived—I'd be able to ID him. He'd either chased me through the woods for that reason, or revenge for his fat friend. I didn't necessarily agree or disagree, I just wanted the son of a bitch caught and brought to justice so I could move on with whatever pieces were left of my life.

One thing that was apparent to everyone, though, was that my attackers had never intended me to leave that ditch alive. Bottom line was that Ian's buddy—whoever he was— wanted me dead, and that posed a problem for me to go on with *"life as usual,"* for the time being.

I didn't blame him for wanting me dead. Because once I got my bearings—once I got a minute to *breathe*—I was going to come after him. I was going to do my own investigating and find the bastard. He was not going to get away with ruining my life, or another woman's for that matter.

Tomorrow, though. Tomorrow I'd head home, re-evaluate, assess, and tackle the new day.

Right then, I needed a second. Just a second, to... *be.*

Enter Cabin 1. My hideout, my refuge, where I'd be staying until BSPD caught the guy, or, I got my Jeep back and could skip town for a while. I didn't know. All I knew right then was that I needed a place to stay for the night.

Cabin 1 was it.

I was beat, emotionally, physically, mentally. Every way a woman could be beat, I was.

I felt physically sick, something that Celeste had picked up on over the last hour, and demanded the police out of the house and for Gage to take me away.

He did.

We didn't speak as we walked down the pathway, pine needles crunching under the fuzzy slippers Celeste had given me after Gage tended to my feet. I inhaled the crisp, autumn air in an attempt to clear my head from the fog that was creeping up. It smelled like moldy fallen leaves, and death.

The trail took a curve and Gage lightly grabbed my hand and led me to a shiny side-by-side ATV. I didn't ask where exactly we were going, I didn't care.

He helped me into the passenger seat, guiding me softly, with hands along my back. Usually that would rub me the wrong way. At that moment, I would have let him pick me up and lay me in it. No time, no energy for any kind of feminist pissing matches at that moment.

If I'm being totally honest, I would have preferred to be laid on that little spot on his chest instead of inside the ATV.

With a low rumble of the engine, we started through the dark woods, down a manicured rock trail with landscaping along the sides. Swaying moonbeams danced along the forest floor as we journeyed deeper into the brush, an eerie, blue glow lighting our way.

A gust of wind sent a shiver down my spine and I wrapped my arms around myself.

Gage pulled a camo Carhartt jacket from the back.

"Thanks," my voice barely audible as he handed it to me.

We drove for another few minutes in silence, bumping over the rocks, my body numb to the sensation. Then, he looked over at me, dappled moonlight dancing across his face.

"You did good in there."

Was any other way acceptable?

A few seconds passed. "Where exactly is Cabin 1?"

"Just down the hill, not far. It's where you'll be staying for the next week."

"What?" My neck snapped to him. *"Week? No, no, Gage.* I'm going home tomorrow. I have a *job.* I can't just... "

"Don't worry about the cost. It's covered."

The *cost?* My lethargy was suddenly replaced by— perhaps a bit misplaced—raw anger.

"What the hell's that supposed to mean?"

"It means you're still in danger and you need personal security until the threat is neutralized."

"You'll cover the cost?" My emotions began to spin inside me like a hurricane. "You just automatically think I can't take care of myself? Because I was beat up? Physically weak and financially weak? Is that it?"

"Cool it, sweetheart." A little sharp attitude of his own.

"Don't call me sweetheart."

"Don't piss me off, Miss Avery."

"It's *Niki,* and don't tell me what to do. I'll do whatever the hell I want. I don't have to be here, you know." My tone was like a spoiled, defiant child's. "In fact, I'll just *walk* home."

My body flew forward as he slammed the brake. I had to grab the side to keep from falling out... which was exactly his intention, I think.

"No, you don't have to be here." He spit out. "And I'm sure as hell not going to try to convince you of it anymore. You go, he gets you, that's on you then, sweetheart. Get on out, then. I'll get back to my beer. Doesn't make a goddamn difference to me."

My eyebrows raised as I glowered at him, the spark in his eye as hot as my own. This guy could give as good as got, and probably more—pretty face or not. I wasn't used to that. Or, maybe I hadn't been around a real tough-guy. No,

Gage Steele didn't tolerate being snapped at, or stupidity for that matter, because of course I wasn't going to go home. He knew that. He didn't tolerate pointless arguing, and was willing to throw me out on the curb—or onto the ground—despite the electricity shooting between us.

I realized then that I was dealing with a loose cannon. Erratic. Someone hot tempered, like me. Gage Steele and I were going to be like gasoline and fire. We were either going to keep a safe distance from each other, or explode. Together.

I gave in first, tearing my eyes away from him. He waited, still staring at me, challenging me to say another word. When he was satisfied I'd shut up for good, he continued down the trail with a jolt—scaring me—and jarring the silence that had settled between us.

I couldn't control myself then. I gripped the sides and scowled at him, my pulse quickening with anger. It felt good to argue, to fight, to release tension. So I went in. Hard.

"You think the only reason I want to go home is because I don't have the means for protection?" I cackled a laugh that made me sound like a hysterical, crazed woman. Which, at the moment, wasn't too far from the truth. "I have plenty of money, and plenty of means of protection. I have a gun at my house, but who the hell needs a gun? Right? *Right?*" I was spinning. "Just give me a freaking steak knife." My voice pitched, cracked. "I *killed* a man tonight, Gage. I *killed* a *man.*" With that, the tears exploded out of me, an uncontrollable wave of emotions hitting me with the force of a thousand bricks. I broke. I mean completely, utterly, snot dripping from my nose broke down.

Moments passed with me sobbing with my face in my hands, then, I noticed we'd stopped.

"No," I whispered between sobs. "Just... please, get me to wherever I'm going, and let me be. Leave me alone."

"Niki..." his low, smooth voice whispered back. "Niki, come here."

I didn't. I couldn't. I was embarrassed, shaken to the core, and *obviously* not thinking straight.

Instead, I continued to cry, and he let me, until I felt his hand slide onto my leg. Then, a finger on my chin. He lifted, turning my head to him, where he'd gotten out of the ATV and walked to the passenger side. To my side. He was squatted, looking up at me, his stormy eyes reflecting in the moonlight.

"Don't cry," he whispered again. "Please. Don't cry."

I heard the words, but between the uncontrollable release I was having, I didn't stop. Couldn't. I swatted his hand away.

He gave me another minute, then touched my arm, softly, asking for approval. When I didn't jerk away, he added the other. I felt him move closer, and God I wanted him closer. I wondered if I'd said my thoughts out loud because the next second, I was wrapped into his arms and pulled to the ground with him. The solid earth felt good beneath me, stable. The man felt good against me as I cried into his leather jacket. An anchor, a strength, a calm against a night of total chaos. He stroked my head, listened to me cry, not asking any questions, not asking for anything in return, until finally, finally, there were no more tears.

Nothing left of me.

It was as if my body had been rung of every emotion a human being could have, and I'd turned into nothing more than a hollow shell.

A hollow shell of the woman I used to be.

Sucking in my snot, I wiped my nose, my cheeks, then scrubbed my face with my hands.

He helped me stand.

I couldn't look at his face.

No words were spoken as he helped me back into the ATV, then continued down the path until we veered to the left, onto another narrow path. This one wound deeper through the forest, thicker trees and underbrush, and I took the time to breathe deeply in a desperate attempt to recenter myself. And I wondered if that was even possible.

Up ahead, I spotted golden lights twinkling through the trees. Another corner, then the path faded into a clearing with a small log cabin aglow through the darkness. It reminded me of one of those Thomas Kinkade paintings. Warm, welcoming, quaint, complete with a chimney and wraparound porch. Colorful potted mums lined the steps. Fallen leaves speckled the roof and ground, the moon resting on the peak.

"Cabin 1?"

Gage nodded. "Ready?"

Breath escaped me in an exasperated display. I had nothing. No bag to take in with me, no phone, no clothes, nothing. Only a single red leaf tucked into the waistband of my shorts.

Nodding, I dragged myself out of the ATV, my body like a limp noodle. I looked around as I crossed the rock driveway that disappeared somewhere down the hill. Dense woods hugged the cabin, providing privacy, and extra security if I had to guess.

"You okay?"

I hadn't realized Gage was watching me.

I nodded and met him at the front door. No key, just a

numbered keypad that demanded a ridiculously long code, and Gage's fingerprint to enter.

The thick wooden door opened to a single room, decorated with lush, dark leather furniture and plaid blankets, and a bookshelf with more books than I could read in a lifetime. It smelled fresh and clean, like Pine Sol, with a hint of vanilla. The lights had already been turned on. Not heavy fluorescent overhead lights, but soft, table and floor lamps casting a golden glow across the room. A wall of windows, black with night, looked out to an observatory deck overlooking the woods. To the right, a small kitchen with upscale appliances and the same copper cookware as the main house. The left wall was lined with a beautiful stone fireplace, flanked by two rooms. One a small bedroom with four-poster bed and blinding white comforter that looked as light and fluffy as a cloud, the other, a dark stone bathroom with a copper soaking tub and sink.

"It's beautiful." And it was.

Gage made his way into the kitchen.

My gaze landed on a large bag with a note that read *Niki,* sitting on the coffee table.

"Let me guess? Tampons and itch-cream?"

Gage grinned as he checked the windows and locks. "No clue. Celeste got the room ready. I'm guessing it's clothes, over-priced girly showering stuff, and whatever lotions and goo you guys use while getting ready. Let me show you around."

I followed him through the cabin as he walked me through the appliances, the fridge that was fully stocked, the automatic fireplace, the bedroom, the bathroom. Lastly, and most importantly, he showed me the security system, complete with a remote control the size of a jumbo cell phone, with all the bells and whistles of one.

"No one can get inside this cabin. We have bullet proof windows, walls, and security cameras throughout the mountain. Shit goes down..." he paused. "'Scuse the language."

A smile tugged my lips. "Don't worry about that with me. Thank you, though."

"Okay then, glad we got that out of the way. Anyway, if shit goes down, you're safe."

A tiny bit of tension released from my shoulders. "What if I want to go outside?"

"You'll need to press your code to deactivate the alarm. When you go back in, you'll reactivate it. If you forget, don't worry, it reactivates every twenty minutes, and will give you a courtesy beep if you're still outside, in which case you'll have to deactivate it again."

"What about a phone? I don't have one. How will I get ahold of you?"

He stepped over to the fireplace, pulled down an ornate turquoise box from the mantle and lifted a small necklace. It was beautiful. Somehow, I knew that wasn't the point, though. He lifted it over my head, like a King to his Knight. Gage the King, me his servant. The second time that evening I'd felt that. Resigning, I dipped my chin as he slid it around my neck. He swept the hair away from my shoulder, his thumb brushing my cheek. A wave of tingles flew over my skin. I looked up, into eyes that were staring down at me with such intensity that my heart skipped a beat. His gaze shifted to the knot below my eye. The muscle in his jaw twitched, then, he looked back at me. Eyes locked, he leaned forward, and for a moment I thought he might kiss me. Instead, he secured the clasp on the back of my neck, whispering in my ear, "You'll wear this while you're here." The warmth of his breath, the proximity of his lips had my pulse thrumming. "There's a small button on the backside of the pendent. Push it if you need me, if you ever get scared, and I'll be right there." He pulled away, taking the scorching heat between us with him. Like the pull of a magnet, I could actually feel the sexual tension vibrating between us.

Like fire and gasoline.

"Where will you be?" I whispered, not sure why.

"The main house." He narrowed his eyes with that intensity that I was learning was simply a part of him. "I'll be here if you need me. You can count on that."

I nodded and began turning the pendant over in my fingers. "Thank you, Gage."

He scanned my face, settling on my lips.

I worried he could hear the drum of my heart through the silence.

Finally, he met my gaze, tilted his head. "What's with the leaf?"

"Oh." My hand dropped to the waistband of my shorts, my eyes to the floor. "It's..." I covered the leaf with my hand wondering how to explain its symbolism, especially to a man. How to explain that the little leaf had saved my life. That little leaf symbolized strength. Survival.

I couldn't explain it, then, anyway, so I didn't. "It's just something I picked up." I lifted my face to his, cocking a brow.

He nodded, and I saw that understanding in his face again. The same understanding when he'd realized exactly how I'd been attacked.

He pulled a pair of dog tags from under his shirt.

"What are those?"

"... Just something I picked up."

I smiled, fighting the urge to lean up on my tiptoes and kiss him.

He tucked his necklace under his shirt. "I'll make sure Opal knows not to throw it away."

"Opal?"

"Housekeeping."

Of course.

"Thank you."

He ran his finger down the bruise on my face. "Niki, I just want you to know…"

A screaming cell phone interrupted him. He quickly stepped back, the heat dissolving from his eyes, and seamlessly switched back to all-business as he read a text message.

"I've got to go. Your personal security code is 4764. Randomly generated. Myself and my brothers know it, no one else does. It resets with every tenant. Are you hungry?"

"Okay, and, no… not yet any way."

"There's plenty of food in the fridge, or if you want anything else, we can get it for you. The main house number is on the phone in the bedroom, along with my personal cell. Call if you need anything. You've got a golf cart parked on the side of the cabin. Feel free to come to the main house anytime. Follow the trail out the back. The driveway heads down the mountain to the main dirt road; don't take that, always take the back trails. And always take your necklace, and don't forget to set the alarms. Lastly, no one is allowed to wander the grounds after nightfall."

I glanced out the window, unbelieving of where I was, and what I was listening to. I was officially someone who needed personal security.

"Niki…"

I shifted my empty gaze back to my protector.

"You're safe here. You have my word." As if he couldn't resist another touch, he swept a strand of hair from my face.

"I won't let anything happen to you. You're safe, and you're not alone."

You're not alone.

I dipped my chin as the sting of tears threatened to give me away. I didn't want to cry in front of him. Not again.

Taking the cue, he stepped back, hesitating a moment before turning and walking out the front door.

And leaving me with my tears.

11

NIKI

*M*y eyes popped open to darkness and panic seized me. I didn't know where I was, or what I was doing there. My gaze darted around the room, desperately trying to pull memories. I zeroed in on a red, flashing light from a phone on the end of the couch that I'd fallen asleep on. Except it wasn't a phone, it was a security remote.

A security remote for the cabin I'd been swept away to in an attempt to save my life from the man who wanted to take it.

My stomach rolled with the memories.

I sat up, pain shooting up my back as the soft Navajo-print afghan fell to the hardwood floor below me. A cool breeze swept over my once warmed skin as I looked at the windows, inky-black with night.

I looked at the clock—2:47 a.m.

Hours away from light. Hours away from a new day to start over, begin fresh. The start of many long, difficult roads that now laid ahead of me. One road, finding the son of a bitch who tried to kill me, and dealing with the gossip that would come with it. One road navigating my job, and figuring out if, God willing, being a sexual assault victim wouldn't affect my position. Lastly, one road, and perhaps the most difficult of all, trying to heal and forget. Although, I knew in my heart I would never fully heal, and I sure as hell would never forget. It would become a part of me—for better or worse. They say what doesn't kill you makes you stronger. I guessed I was about to find out, but one thing I knew for certain was that my life had changed forever.

A life I'd worked so damn hard to build into a meaningful one, with the promise of a prosperous future where I didn't have to depend on anyone or anything. Truly independent, that was always my goal. From the moment that I was born into poverty in a rusted, stained bathtub—one of the few facts that had never reached the Berry Springs gossips—I'd fought for dignity. Most people fought for respect, for honor, for a clean slate. No, I fought for dignity. Screw money, screw name-brand clothes, new athletic shoes, snacks, screw all that stuff. All I wanted was to have self-respect. Pride. I believed I was more than how I was brought into this world. And I was. Dammit, I was.

Even in the shadows behind the bleachers where the giggles followed me like an incurable plague, I had faith in myself. I studied. I read. I taught myself three different languages... what I was going to do with Gaelic, I wasn't sure, but Spanish had proved to serve me well. I graduated valedictorian of my class, although no one remembered that. I got a full ride to college and worked my ass off to obtain a double degree. All that paled in comparison to passing the bar exam. Now my career was up in the air. My name would be all over the local news, all over the local diners, hair salons. The fact that I had been sexually assaulted would surely leak out. My name—the name I'd worked so damn hard to build up—would be tarnished.

Again.

Feeling nauseous, I pushed off the couch. I could handle emotional pain and torment. Not feeling sick on top of that. So, in a desperate attempt to ease an ounce of my discomfort, I padded to the kitchen. Relieving low blood sugar from lack of food was one thing I could control—something I could fix, right then. On my own. That little thought, that tiny little burst of positivity, sent my stomach growling.

One thing at a time. Fix one thing at a time.

The luxury slippers that my new best friend—aka Celeste—had left for me slid along the hardwood floors, squeezing my aching feet like a warm hug. Her 'welcome bag' didn't disappoint. Inside were several changes of clothes—all the correct sizes—including a gray Steele Shadows T-shirt made of the softest cotton I'd ever felt, and flannel bottoms, thick and cozy, both I had slipped into the moment Gage had left. Also inside the bag was an impressive selection of makeup, hair products, a journal, and a jumbo bag of M&M's... the necessities for any woman on the run.

As I walked to the kitchen, I scanned the thick log walls, the nature paintings that hung on them, the antique light fixtures, and wondered how many people had spent evenings inside that exact cabin. What path had their lives taken to lead them to that point? Was it safe to assume everyone had been attacked in one way or another? If not physically, perhaps emotionally? They'd been brought there to sort out the pieces of their lives while someone, or something, threatened to take it away?

It was a haunting thought.

Less haunting than realizing I had become one of them.

The thought was like a shot of espresso to my system, jolting me into the same vibrating anxiety I'd felt before exhaustion had gripped me and pulled me under, if only for a few hours.

No way was I going back to sleep.

I yanked open the fridge, stocked with fresh fruits, veggies, meats, cheeses, and in the freezer, pizzas, ice cream, and a stack of organic insta-dinners. I grabbed an apple, stick of cheese, and decaffeinated soda—something light, something to fill the void in my stomach. I leaned against the counter and nibbled, my gaze drifting outside where the full moon washed over the mountains. A cluster of lights twinkled through the trees. The main house.

Gage.

He was awake. Apparently, the whole house was.

A ripple of butterflies swept through my empty stomach at the mere thought of the man. Of his touch on my legs, the tip of his finger on my face, that damn look in his eyes that sent every sexual sensor zipping to attention.

I'd heard about the Steele brothers—real bad boys, tough as nails, and even tougher to tame. Former Marines who'd recently left the military to take over their father's business after he'd passed away. Rumor was they rarely left their compound, except to go to the local bar, a trip that more often than not ended in a fist fight... and except to take home the random women they'd picked up during the occasion. Rumor was they were decidedly—not tragically— single. Very single, playboys, each having many women, but never letting one get too close.

Each willing to die for the other.

Rumor was, the Steele family was thick as thieves.

I wondered what Gage was doing. Finishing that beer? Watching television? Snuggling with a busty blonde?

Keeping my focus on the house in the distance, I pushed out the back door onto the deck. A series of angry beeps whirled through the silence, reminding me to grab the security remote and type in the code Gage had written down on a post-it before he'd left. His handwriting, by the way, was as aggressive and sharp as every word that came out of his mouth. Quick slashes of letters as if it pained him to even take the second to write it.

The heavy wooden door closed behind me. A porch swing surrounded by candles and yellow and orange mums swayed in the cool air, its shadow dancing along the deck floor. Dead leaves tumbled across my slippers. The night was quiet, eerily so.

Taking a deep breath, I walked to the railing. My hand mindlessly drifted to the security necklace around my neck, and I lightly rubbed the *SOS* button on the back.

Another deep breath, inhaling the fresh, clean mountain air, then I leaned my elbows against the railing and stared at the castle on the hill.

What would it be like to live like that? To have everything in the world at your fingertips, or at least the money to get it there. To be impossibly handsome, rich, powerful... lethal. My thoughts drifted again to his hands on my legs, slowly cleaning my wounds. Slowly igniting a fire inside me.

I felt a tingle below, heat, an unfamiliar need beginning to warm my skin.

I looked at the number he'd taped to the back of the remote. *His* number.

I glanced back at the wireless phone sitting on the coffee table. Maybe—

Crack!

My heart slammed against my ribcage as a bullet whizzed past my head, so close my hair flew up with the break of wind. Panic shot through me like lightning as I lunged to the side, diving onto the deck floor.

Another *crack,* sounding like a bomb exploding in the distance. A flower pot shattered inches from my head. Dirt flew everywhere, all over me, as bullets pinged off the windows behind me. I desperately grabbed for my necklace, which had twisted around my neck, dangling somewhere down my back.

I couldn't scream, couldn't breathe, couldn't think. I was in complete terror as my head spun like a top.

The rope of the necklace burned my skin as I yanked it around my neck to find the button.

Another shot, splitting the wood railing in front of my forehead, and I knew the shooter had me solidly in his sights now.

I was screwed. He'd come back for me, and he was going to finish the job.

I braced for impact just as a body flew through the air, barreling me into the corner a split-second before the bullet pierced my forehead.

Gage.

Gasping for breath, I was pinned underneath him, every inch of his body covering mine. He was yelling to someone, or into something perhaps. I couldn't make out the words.

I cranked my head to the side and blinked, clearing my blurred vision as my eyes darted around the deck floor.

And my stomach rolled like a wave.

Beneath spikey hair matted with leaves and dried blood, a pair of frozen eyes stared lifelessly into my soul, a tongue hanging grotesquely out of a grayish-blue mouth, opened slightly as if he was trying to tell me something. And just below that, bloody strings of skin dangled from the decapitated head of Ian Lee.

12

NIKI

"Shots coming from the northwest corner of the property, check the cliff." Gage's booming voice faded in and out through the erratic pumping of my heart.

His body shifted off of me as he frantically looked me over. "Are you okay?"

I swallowed the bile in my throat. *"Ian's..."* I squeaked out. "Gage, *look.*"

He followed my gaze, coolly assessed the decapitated head as if it weren't the first he'd seen, then, focused back on me. "Are *you* okay?"

"Yes. *Gage,* the *head.*"

"Don't touch it. We leave it exactly where it is for the police. Celeste has already called them. You're sure you're not hurt?"

"Yes."

He slid his arms underneath me and swept me off the deck, as more gunfire popped in the distance.

He carried me into the cabin. "Well, maybe they got him."

"Who? Who got him?"

"My brothers."

I was carried to the kitchen and slid onto the counter, for the second time that evening. Something about counters, apparently.

"I couldn't get to my necklace in time... I'm sorry... how did you know I needed you? How..."

"I was in the woods." He scanned my body as if he didn't believe I wasn't hurt.

"In the woods doing what?"

"Watching you." His gaze flickered to me, then back to a small cut he'd found on my knee. He pulled a bandage from the counter and ripped off the top with his teeth.

"Watching me? At almost three in the morning?"

"Every second of the day. That's my job, Niki."

My heart fluttered and I didn't know if it was because of the sting of the antiseptic wipe, or the fact that Gage had never really left me.

Even if it were only his job.

"Did you see whoever left... it?"

He clenched his jaw. "No, must've done it earlier while we were still up at the house."

My mouth dropped. "Meaning, he never left the area..."

Icy eyes narrowed. "Exactly."

"Meaning... he didn't give up." My stomach rolled at the thought. I was being stalked.

Just then, the rumble of an ATV stopped outside the back door, followed by heavy footsteps onto the deck.

"That'll be Ax. Stay put."

Gage secured the bandage then disappeared into the living room. I jumped off the counter as his as-strikingly-handsome twin brother entered the cabin.

"Get him?" Gage asked Ax.

"No. He had a solid three minute jump on me. Took the

shots from the cliff, exactly like you said, then caught a hunter's trail and took off on a four-wheeler down the mountain. Followed him until the trails crossed. Guy's gone. Wolf is pulling up the cameras."

"What were the shots we heard, then?"

A cocky smile eerily similar to the one I'd seen on Gage a few times crossed Ax's lips. "Just telling him to have a nice evening." He glanced at me, then back to Gage. "Gunner's already out on the roads. Don't know where the hell Feen is."

"Okay. Keep me updated."

"You got it. Cops are on their way." Another glance in my direction, this one laced with a hint of warning, before he disappeared out the front door. A warning to stay inside the cabin? Or a warning to stay away from Gage?

Eyebrow cocked, Gage turned to me. "I told you to stay in the kitchen. Not good at following directions, are we?"

"One of my many charming qualities."

His gaze skimmed my body. Butterflies, again.

"Nice shirt." He leveled on the logo across my chest, or maybe my chest only.

"Courtesy of Celeste."

"Figured." He narrowed his eyes, his jaw twitching. "We need to talk. Sit."

"Listen." I held up a hand. "Thank you. Thank you for taking me in from the woods, thank you for protecting me, and thank you for just saving my life—"

"Why do I feel like there's a but coming?"

"*But* you should know that along with not following directions, another one of my charming qualities is that I'm not a fan of being bossed around..." I paused. "Whether being indebted to you, or not."

He stared with an expression I couldn't quite read. Then,

closed the distance between us, stopping inches from my face, trailing from my eyes, down my cheeks, to my lips, to my hair. I froze in place, my body's response to the proximity of him. To the demanding presence of him. To the *alpha* of him. How many women did he have that effect on, I wondered.

He reached up and slowly pulled a flower petal out of my hair, running it along my earlobe, the touch of his fingertip like electric silk along my neck.

"Niki," his voice low, quiet, ever-demanding of my full attention. "If you were in my debt, believe me, you'd know it."

My heart skipped a beat, and for a split second, I found myself wishing I were in his debt. His servant. His, to do with what he pleased. His, to ravage.

His, his, his.

I stepped back, not because he had inched even closer, but because I feared I wouldn't be able to control my next move. "We need to talk..." I repeated his own comment in an attempt to cool the heat scorching the earth between us.

He blinked as if he hadn't heard a word out of my mouth.

"Yes," he finally said. "We do need to talk." Then, with a twinkle in his grey eyes and a small curve on his lips, he said, "Miss Avery, *ma'am,* may I *please* ask you to take a seat while we have this discussion?"

My eye roll was so dramatic I felt it in my already stabbing headache. I looked at the couch—the last place I needed to be next to this man. Then, at the kitchen. "Actually, I could use a drink."

"Music to my ears. There's whiskey in the cabinet above the fridge."

I looked up at the small cupboard I hadn't even noticed.

"We like to keep it out of reach of clients who aren't regular drinkers, but available for those who need it."

"And know where to look, apparently." I extended onto my tiptoes.

"I'll get it." He breezed past me, that damn mixture of pine and fresh soap tickling my nose again. It was as if the guy knew every trick in the book to knock a woman off her game.

With two fingers of whiskey and one of those big fancy ice cubes in a short glass, I leaned against the cabinet while Gage watched me with his assessing gaze. Endless questions, endless suspicions, endless heat.

He sipped, straight from the bottle. "So what just happened changes things."

"Uh, *yeah.*"

"Haddix is of the impression your attack was random."

"Yeah, I caught that." I sipped. "You don't believe that."

"No, ma'am."

"You didn't believe it before someone tried to gun me down after leaving a severed head outside my door."

"Right."

"Why?"

"The fact he chased you through the woods after everything, after you killed his buddy... that's not the behavior of a random attack."

I'd thought the same thing a hundred times.

"If he was concerned about you being able to ID him, he would have run, regardless. Maybe taken a few shots, but then got the hell out of there. He wouldn't have stalked you through the woods while his buddy was dead on the side of the road. Scenario one, your attack was planned, and the job wasn't finished. He came back right now to get it done. It's personal."

"Agreed on all counts." I gripped the cold, sweating glass. "And what's scenario two?"

"Niki..." a tone that resembled my father's. A tone I didn't much care for. "Are you sure you didn't know them? Or, maybe—"

"Or, maybe *what?*" I snapped.

"Maybe... things got a bit out of hand tonight and you ran."

The instant rage that bubbled up was unprecedented. I'd never been so mad, so quickly in my entire life. Not only because of the accusation that I was lying, because of the gall of it, from *him.* What the *hell* did I owe this guy? Absolutely nothing. He said it himself he'd just been doing his job.

"Scenario two is that I'm lying, right? That you don't believe me." Hand trembling, I set down my drink.

His expression didn't break. He simply stared back at me. Demanding, demanding, demanding.

I was *irate.* I crossed my arms over my chest. "I *know* you, Gage Steele—"

"You don't know shit about me." The venom was back.

"I know plenty about you." I bowed up for the fight, more than ready. "A spoiled rich kid who grew up with a silver spoon in his mouth. Having more than enough, more than needed. More than any kid should have. Always getting your way, always looking down on others from your castle in the sky. I'd say you pitied those *less fortunate* than you, but having met you now, I don't think that's the case. I think you simply didn't even notice. I think you couldn't give a damn about others, or their situation in life. This is all a job to you. You don't care about your clients. No, Gage, *you* don't know *me.*"

His jaw clenched, the only movement in the statue standing across of me.

I continued and began pacing the room like a tiger about to escape its cage. "How dare you insinuate that I'm lying about something like sexual assault? Do you know how many similar cases I've studied and worked on? You think I'm a liar because of my Dad. Let's get one thing straight, *Gage*—I am not my father. I am not my family. I've spent my entire life running away from the way I was raised. Worked my ass off. And for you to think I'd throw it all away for what? Some sort of pity party? For attention? I *hate* attention, Gage. It's my biggest challenge in my job. I don't like standing up in front of people, all eyes on me."

"Why do you do it then?"

I stopped on a dime. "Because I *believe* in it. I'm part of helping people dig their way out of the darkest times in their lives. I want to help them. Get them justice." I paused, cocked my head. "Do you believe in right and wrong? Evil and good? Or is life just a whirling tornado, let us fall where we may."

"I believe we make our own luck."

"Wrong. Sometimes shit happens. Sometimes life happens and throws you down a path you never expected. What's next? You deal with it. And what helps? Having the best team of people around you." I jerked my drink off the counter punctuating my last sentence. "And for you to think I've worked up some story... like my Dad." My voice cracked, the sting of tears heating my eyes. I will them away. "You owe me an apology." When he didn't, I snorted and shook my head. "Ah, screw it." I slammed down my drink, turned my back to him and began walking out of the kitchen. "I don't need this bullshit right now. I'm getting out of here—"

My body jerked back with the force of his grab. I was

spun around like a rag doll and met with a gaze so intense, my heart leapt into my throat.

The grip on my shoulders tightened as he leaned down and crushed his lips onto mine. I was shocked, stunned, once again frozen where I stood, completely under his command, his dominance, exactly how he wanted it. His tongue met mine, a warm tingle of whiskey. My knees buckled, my stomach swam with emotions.

I submitted.

Dammit, I submitted.

Melting into his kiss, I was backed up, stumbling. He effortlessly caught me and pinned me against the wall with a force that knocked the air out of my lungs.

A picture dropped and shattered on the floor.

His grip released, his hands softly cupping my face, kissing, kissing, kissing, until what seemed like only seconds later, he pulled away.

My eyes didn't immediately open. I didn't want them to. I wanted to stay in that moment for the rest of my life. My breath was fast, my heartbeat faster.

I finally opened my eyes, to meet his, his chest rising and falling just as heavily as my own.

"Apologize," I demanded in a breathless whisper.

"No shot in hell," he whispered back, like he was about to devour every inch of me.

I stepped forward. Calmly, coolly, the opposite of the storm that was—is—Gage Steele. Closing in the inches between us, I pushed up to my tiptoes, grabbed a fistful of his shirt and kissed him again. Softly. Slowly. He didn't move, didn't touch, just kissed me back.

My tongue explored his mouth, then ran along his lower lip.

"Apologize," I whispered against his lips. I could feel his heart beating through his chest.

"No." He huskily whispered back.

I didn't move, simply angled my face so that my lips touched the corner of his mouth, the tip of my nose against his check.

"Apologize," I repeated.

"I'm sorry," he said.

13

GAGE

*W*hat. *The fuck.* Was that?

I blinked, because that was the only thing that seemed to be working at that exact moment, aside from the raging boner in my pants.

I struggled to think of the last time I'd apologized to anyone. Especially a woman. I'm sure there were a few here and there—slip-ups, I mean. And by slip-ups, I mean apologies. I never apologized. People dealt with me, with us—my brothers—or they didn't. And if they didn't, well, they could leave. Go straight to hell.

When Niki Avery told me she was going to leave—and she had every reason and right to—it was as if my body took over my brain in a desperate attempt to keep her close. True to form, I didn't think, didn't consider the consequences, just took action. An action that ended up being the best fucking kiss I'd ever had in my life, along with the most ball-busting —correction ball-*removing*—moment of my life.

She'd demanded that I apologize to her.

And... I did.

Jesus. Christ. I did.

My eyes shifted toward the floor, looking at the metaphorical armor this woman had single-handedly stripped from me with one flick of her tongue. I willed myself to step back. I couldn't. Instead, I looked into those deep brown eyes, sparkling with passion... and victory.

And goddammit if the only thing I wanted to do was scoop her up and take her to bed and screw her brains out, making her little victory that much sweeter. For both of us.

Little victory. She knew it was much more than that. The woman knew exactly what had just happened, while, me? All I knew was that I felt like I'd been bent over and taken it up the ass.

Fuck me, I liked it.

The truth was, I had to test her. I had to know for myself that this woman wasn't lying. That she wasn't her dad. I got my answer, I just didn't expect to be neutered in the process.

She didn't thank me for apologizing, no that wasn't this woman's style. Instead, she stepped away from me, sauntered back to the kitchen, grabbed her drink, and downed it in one sip.

I was officially in love.

"Now," she said, leaning against the counter, her voice stronger, more confident—as she should be. "Let's figure out who the hell is trying to kill me."

Well, that was a task I was much better equipped to handle than the one that had just happened, so I crossed the room, grabbed my own drink and leaned against the counter in front of her.

"First," I said, biting back the words *'assuming you are telling the truth now'*, because we all knew how that was going to turn out. "We start from the beginning of the night. You're sure you didn't notice anyone at the yoga retreat looking at you more than usual, perhaps someone who kept grabbing your attention?"

"Yes, I'm sure."

"What about someone that stood out to you? Your gut instinct, your sixth sense pulling you to him. A little red flag."

"I'm positive. Like I told Haddix, it was mostly women, and the men..." she shook her head. "They weren't built like the two guys who attacked me. Those were big guys. Big, drunk guys. Even the skinnier one was bulky. Fit."

"Big, drunk guys don't usually attend yoga?"

She grinned. "No. Not every male has to be drunk to agree to go to a yoga class, Gage."

I smirked. "Okay, so then it had to be someone who either followed you, or knew you were going. *Think,* Niki."

"I'm telling you, no one knew I was going."

"No friends, nothing?"

"No."

"Why?"

"Why, what?"

"Why is that? No friends?"

She shifted her weight and looked down. A sensitive subject. Perhaps more painful than what happened that evening.

"I... ah..." she stammered, then blew out a breath and yanked her shoulders back. A *fuck-you* in response to her moment of weakness. A little tick that was quickly becoming one of my favorite things about her. I poured her another finger of whiskey.

"I know that you know I wasn't popular in school, to say the least," she said. "In those situations, you're forced to rely only on yourself. Become your own best friend. I had to learn at a very early age to accept things I couldn't control.

Like bullies. I hardened myself to it. I guess that carried over into adulthood. Shaped me. And that's fine. That's who I am. It is what it is."

It is what it is.

She tilted her head to the side. "You know, I might ask the same thing about you. Rumor is you and your brothers never leave this place, and when you do its only to hit the bar, together."

"So?"

"So, right back at you—why no friends?"

"You're an only sibling, right?"

"Stop deflecting, and yes."

This girl had spunk. I loved it. "Well, Ax and I are only two minutes apart, Gunner, two years older, and Phoenix, three. We're all close in age."

"That's not the only reason."

I cocked a brow. "Are you analyzing me, Miss Avery?"

"Oh, we don't have all night."

I laughed at this.

"No, being close in age is not the only reason you all are so close, so exclusive."

I sipped, contemplating my answer. "We joined the military together."

"Go on..."

I sipped again, a damn big gulp, and cleared my throat. "Listen, you grew up without much, I grew up with a lot. And whether you believe it or not, there's a certain amount of seclusion that comes with both. Not many people understand it... it makes you different. Feel different, anyway. Your assessment of me, Niki, is off. Way off. I do care about others, and I do care about my clients, I'm just not great at showing it. I know that." Another sip. "My brothers and I have spent fifteen years fighting next to each other, taking care of each other. Killing for each other. Only those who lived it understand it. Period. It's a bond, an unbreakable bond like nothing else in this world."

"The things you've done, together, it's hardened you. Tainted you."

Yes, it had. I knew it had. All of us.

"There's a lot of evil in this world. Tonight, you saw some of that. Niki, I've seen more than that, tenfold. Life is... fragile. Temporary. If you get too attached to something... to anything... to *someone*..." I cleared my throat again and looked down. Uncomfortable didn't begin to describe what I was feeling at that moment. I never opened up. To anyone.

Ever.

I glanced out the window at the house in the distance, still glowing with life despite the fact that it was pushing four in the morning. It always was that way. We never slept.

"And," I exhaled, clearing that conversation. "The company is a lot of work."

She slowly nodded, staring at me, those midnight eyes piercing into my soul. "I'm sorry about your dad."

I raised the bottle and took a sip. A heavy moment passed.

"So," she said, her voice cheery, lighthearted, and for that, I was thankful. "The infamous Steele brothers, loners and lovers, then."

A smile crossed my lips, a nonverbal thank-you for changing the subject.

She dipped her chin in acknowledgement. Not twelve hours did I know that woman and we were already tuned into each other's nonverbal. Wasn't sure if that made me uncomfortable or not.

I set the bottle down. "Loners and lovers, huh? Is that the word on the street?"

"Oh, yeah. You guys are legendary for one-night stands."

"Not a lot of complications." I tested her.

"... Easy marks." She sipped, watching me over the rim. "No hard work involved, just a few well-timed glances and thinly veiled attempts to avoid any kind of serious conversation. Don't let her get too close."

"That's right." I squared my shoulders and delivered the true test. "Is that something you can handle, Niki?"

Her eyes squeezed into a thin line. "No shot in hell."

The words lingered in the air like a lead weight.

Like a challenge.

We stared at each other, the electricity all but exploding around us. She sipped again, a small droplet of whiskey sliding down her chin, sending the blood funneling between my legs. It took every bit of restraint I had not to throw the drink across the floor, toss her onto the counter and spear into her with the force of an electromagnetic railgun.

Her eyes twinkled, knowing exactly what she was doing to me.

She looked away, focusing on the window. "Anyway, back to the subject at hand. There's a chance I was followed, I guess, although I'd certainly like to think I'd notice."

I took a silent breath, trying to cool my thoughts and focus on the real issue here—that someone was trying to kill Niki Avery, not the missile in my pants.

"Most people don't notice when they're being followed, trust me."

"You do a lot of following, Gage?"

"Only for something I want."

"Good to know," she grinned then continued, "So, let's assume I was followed to the retreat. The guys waited until it was over, then started following me..."

"They took side roads which is why you didn't notice."

"Side roads? Around here?

"Yep. This leads me to believe it has to be someone local. So, I'm going to go back to my initial question in the beginning of this whole thing. Can you think of anyone, *anyone* who'd want to hurt you?"

She puffed out a breath and began pacing the room. "I'm telling you, I lead a boring life. No friends, no drama."

"No boyfriends, right?"

Her gaze leveled mine. "That's right."

"Girlfriends?" I grinned and this was met with the world's most dramatic eye roll.

She blew out a breath. "I know how this stuff goes. It's a long road. I've worked countless cases involving assault. Nasty cases."

"Think about those, then. Our firm has handled security cases where lawyers were threatened during a high profile case. They're sitting ducks for it."

Her brows tipped up. "Hadn't even considered that. Good thinking..." She ran her fingers through her hair. I found myself gawking as the silky brown fell down her back.

"God, Gage, I've tried dozens of cases..."

"We need to pull together a list and go through them one by one."

She nodded. "I wish I had my damn laptop. I've got everything on my work computer at my house. Can you take me now?"

"I'll have Ax get it first thing in the morning. I don't want you going anywhere that you'd be expected."

"My house keys—"

"Are in your Jeep. He'll get them. In the meantime, are there any cases that stick out to you? Think back... anyone the same size, same build as your attackers? Anything with Ian Lee?"

"Nothing with Ian." Her face pulled in concentration. "And, no, not that I can think of, right now, anyway. Those files will jog my memory." Her frown deepened. "Whoever it was went to great lengths to scare me. I mean, to decapitate a man and put his head outside my window..."

"I don't think it was only to scare you, Niki."

"What do you mean?"

I let a moment slide by, wondering if she'd come to the same conclusion I had.

She did.

"*Wait.*" Her mouth dropped. "You think it was a message?"

"I do. I think this is personal, and I think it was a threat. I think your attacker thinks you saw him, or recognized him perhaps, *or* there's some sort of connection that he thinks you're going to put together. I think that's why he came back for you."

She began pacing. "But, why *the head?* I mean, why not something else from the scene... anything else. Why Ian's *head?*"

"Did any of the cases you worked involve someone losing a head?" I asked, almost sarcastically.

The blood drained from her face. "Oh my... *God...* The last case I worked... His name was Mickey Greco. He was arrested for tax fraud and multiple perjury charges. His trial lasted for weeks." She covered her mouth with her hand. "Oh, my God, *Gage...*"

"Stop, take a deep breath." I pushed away from the counter as she inhaled, then exhaled. "Now, talk. Tell me about him."

She nodded, spinning a bit less. "He was a typical white

collar stock broker who owned his own financial management firm, but behind the scenes, he was one of the biggest heroin dealers in the state, using his client's funds when he needed it. He was a bad guy, Gage. Rumor was, if you owed him money, he'd go after you, your family, the whole nine yards. Anyway, a few of his firm's clients had gone to the police when their funds had mysteriously run out. I worked with them trying to build a case, for months. The issue was, Mickey was a saint on the surface, squeaky clean. The cops couldn't get anything on him..." Her eyes darkened. "Until his business partner, a woman by the name of Sheila Cancio, was found raped, brutally tortured... and decapitated in her vacation home in Florida." She swallowed the knot in her throat. "His clients think she'd uncovered his drug operation and threatened to go to the cops. She fled to Florida, but couldn't escape him."

Her voice trailed off and she blinked, the realization like a sledgehammer, to both of us. My hands balled to fists as her eyes met mine. Yes, that could have been her. She knew it and I knew it.

She continued, her voice shaky now. "The ME said Sheila was alive for almost all of the attack. She was kept alive for hours, slowly tortured to death." Niki looked down. "She wasn't found for three days."

"Was he charged for her murder?"

"*No.* No, that's the thing. Guy had solid alibis. Multiple alibis, and was even on camera at several places around town during the few days of her presumed death."

"He had someone else do it." She nodded, and I spoke her thoughts. "The same guy who came after you."

"Possibly, yes."

"So what did Mickey get put away for?"

"You know the story of Al Capone? Cops could never pin

him for murder. They got him for tax evasion. You see, after that happened, one of his clients who owed him money came to me."

"Name?"

"David Campos. The police offered him immunity to tell us what he knew. In his testimony, he claimed Mickey broke his fingers with a hammer, one by one, promising worse to come if he didn't get paid. The guy had medical records to back it up, along with a paper trail leading us right to a money laundering operation within Greco's company. That witness was the nail in the coffin, so to speak."

"And that witness came to *you*. And it's safe to say Greco wouldn't have been locked away if not for your witness's testimony, correct?"

She slowly nodded.

"Niki, when was Mickey officially sentenced?"

"... Three days ago."

14

GAGE

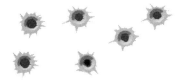

I awoke swinging, my fist making contact with something shiny and light. Something familiar. A beer can.

"Morning, sunshine."

I blinked, a beam of early morning sunlight piercing my retinas like a nuclear laser beam. Squinting, I shifted back into the shadows and sat up on Niki's porch swing. An orchestra of birds chirped around me, reminding me of the headache I'd gone to sleep with... two hours earlier. It was a cool, crisp fall morning, the light breeze scented with a hint of burned leaves. The sun was barely peeking over the mountains, dawn not yet reaching the shaded woods around me. A cloudless sky promised a clear day ahead. I sure as hell hoped so.

With a shit-eating grin, Ax juggled another beer can, ready to launch another attack.

"Bastard," I grumbled, stretching my arms over my head, my back popping in places I didn't even know existed.

"First time a woman kicked you out?" Ax stepped onto

the deck of Cabin 1 and walked over to the porch swing—
my makeshift bed for the evening. "I think I'm liking this
Niki Avery already."

"What time is it?"

"Six-twenty-nine."

"God, why the hell do you have so much energy in the
mornings?" I rolled my neck in a feeble attempt to untangle
the knots. "She didn't kick me out. I voluntarily slept out
here." I glanced over my shoulder into the cabin, still
shrouded in darkness, thankful she was still sleeping. That
was good. She needed sleep.

"Probably for the best, anyway. Feen would have your
hide if you slept with her. You didn't *sleep* with her, did you?"

"Can we please hold off on the Spanish-fucking-inquisi-
tion until I get some coffee?"

Ax folded his arms over his chest.

I rolled my eyes. *"No.* Okay? We didn't *sleep together.*
What are you, a fourth generation deacon in the Baptist
church? Who the hell says *sleep together* anymore?" I raised
up a finger. "No, I'll tell you who. A guy who needs to get
laid, that's who."

"This from the guy who has more condoms than
bullets."

I quickly glanced over my shoulder again.

Ax pounced. "Holy. *Shit.* You *like* her?"

"What's to like?" I grumbled, stretching my neck from
side to side.

Boisterous laughter from my twin.

"Shhh. Dammit, Ax." I stumbled to my feet, holding the
creaking swing quiet as it steadied.

"Fine, I'll back off, but just know, you sleep with this
chick, you might spend the next few months answering

phones. Feen's serious about you getting your head out of your ass."

"Get your head out of your ass."

"And working on your comebacks."

"Fuck you."

"Nice."

I took one last look into the cabin to make sure the light on the alarm system was blinking.

"Come on, Romeo, we've got our Monday morning meeting. Let's go. She's fine."

I hesitated—embarrassing myself in front of my brother. What the hell was wrong with me? I couldn't leave this damn woman. I wasn't thinking straight. Coffee was what I needed, with a little Bailey's and a swift kick in the ass.

I stepped off the deck and joined Ax and switched to work mode, running through any updates I had in my head.

Every Monday since Dad's death, Dallas held, what she called, an *update meeting* about the estate, the business, the week's schedule. She liked to know who was doing what, and where they were doing it. A bit annoying, but we all knew it was her way to attempt to step in and take a portion of Dad's place.

I glanced back at the cabin one last time before we stepped into the woods. "Any updates?"

"Gunner just found the bullet shells on the cliff where the guy camped out. Twenty-two rifle. Clear shot right through the woods to Cabin 1."

My gut clenched. "We need to block that."

"It's on the list."

"Any boot prints or finger prints on the deck?"

"Nope."

I grunted, not surprised. I'd stayed in the cabin with Niki while BSPD made their second journey through the compound, taking statements and canvassing the area. Within the course of a few hours, Niki's case had become number one priority and it was unanimously agreed that her attack was not random. Someone wanted revenge for Mickey Greco, using their buddy's head as a message, a threat. That person was out to kill Niki Avery. And that thought sent my heart slamming and head spinning.

"What did Wolf find on the security cameras?" We stepped onto the trail that led to the main house. My eyes scanned the woods, miles and miles of trees, cliffs, caves, plenty of places to hide. A duo of squirrels darted in front of us sending my hand flexing for the gun on my hip. Not even seven in the morning and I was already as jumpy as a damn chihuahua.

Ax, on the other hand, was as on-point as always. Bastard.

"Our shooter had a black ski mask on—probably same as when he attacked Niki—black gloves and hoodie. Drove a Polaris Sportsman, 450 or 570 Wolf guesses based on the size and features. We've got him coming up from the east side, dropping the head—sick fuck—then heading back down the mountain. Last shot was at the base, before we assume he went up to the cliff. I forwarded the photos to the police. Not a great shot of him, but good of the four-wheeler. They'll look at all recent purchases from local retailers, interview the owners..."

"Why wasn't security tripped?"

"We don't own the *entire* mountain range, Gage. The cliff is just off our land. He skirted around our property."

"Not when he dropped the head. We need to install motion activated alerts around the cabins."

"Tried that, remember? It wasn't worth the time Wolf was having to check the alerts. Everything was setting them off, squirrels, raccoons..." he looked at me with a wicked smirk. "That tattooed blonde that couldn't let go."

I snorted. Man, I'd hooked up with some real winners.

"Besides," he continued. "Our clients come and go as they wish, that's part of the deal. While they're with us, or inside the cabins, they're untouchable. We can put a lock on her." Ax grinned.

A *lock* was when, for special circumstances, we demanded the client not leave the cover of their cabin, not even to take a breath of fresh air. Not even to open a window. They were not allowed to leave, unless sandwiched between my brother and I. It was no fun, for us or for them, and required a lot of man hours, and patience. Something told me that patience was not one of Niki's strong suits.

I exhaled. "What'd we pull up on Mickey Greco?"

"He's still in prison, didn't bust out and come for Niki."

There went my *easy* scenario.

"And he's a model prisoner, I might add. Jagg knows the warden. Spoke to him personally."

"Well, damn. We need to pull a list of everyone who's come to visit him, called, whatever."

"Jagg's on it. Warden's pulling it, owed him a favor."

"And all the names of people that worked at Greco's office. Someone is going to great lengths for revenge. They idolize the bastard. We need to look at family, friends..."

"Done. Wolf pulled together a report. It's on your desk. He also *anonymously* forwarded it to Lieutenant Colson, to which Colson replied by sending us a group text promising a round at Frank's as a thank you."

It was a widely known secret that Steele Shadows Security helped local authorities as much as they helped us. Small town departments with even smaller budgets had to do what they had to do to get things done. And considering we ran a personal security firm in the area, we were only happy to help out. Quid pro quo.

"The guy was on a four wheeler. He has to be a local; has to live around here."

"That doesn't mean shit, Gage. Everyone has a four wheeler around here, and everyone has means to tow it wherever they want. Probably had his truck and trailer parked in a clearing somewhere. You know how many roads snake around these mountains."

"I don't like that lack of faith, Ax."

"Just pointing out the obvious."

"You're always good for that."

"Someone has to be. Anyway, there's a campground along Shadow River thirteen miles south. Gunner already called to see if anyone had a four wheeler. Nada. Gunner also met with Opal, who says she spoke with the staff, none of who claims to have left last night, or saw or heard anything."

I shook my head. "Anything turn up on Niki's Jeep? Prints? Anything?"

"Dude, it's been ten hours. That takes days."

We walked a moment in silence, until I addressed the pink elephant.

"The guy knows where she's staying and doesn't give a shit."

"Burns the hell out of me, too."

"Ballsy mother fucker to come on our land."

"Not a fan of ballsy mother fuckers, Gage."

"Me either, bro. Me either."

We crossed the lawn to the main house and pushed through the back door where we were assaulted with the whining of trumpets echoing off the walls. Smooth jazz instrumental music only meant one thing—Dallas was cooking breakfast. Despite the ear pollution, my mouth watered the moment I smelled the bacon.

"Knew you wouldn't want to miss this," Ax grinned. "Hot chick or not."

"Thanks, smartass."

We rounded the corner into the kitchen, and sure enough, wearing an oversized Billy Idol T-shirt, flannel shorts, and fuzzy eskimo-looking slippers, Dallas flipped a pancake like a pro. She glanced over her shoulder at us, the messy bun of blonde hair bobbing on top of her head.

"Aw, my boys. Good morning." Pride swelled her face.

"Morning, Ma. Smells good." I pecked her on the cheek, eyeing the bag of flax seed on the counter. "Seeds don't go in pancakes, Ma."

"If I've told you once, I've told you a hundred times, Gage, you need to eat better. Flax has protein and all sorts of goodies in it. How many eggs you want?"

"Four."

"Five, then. You too, Ax?"

"Yes, ma'am."

I grabbed a mug, filling it to the brim with piping hot coffee from a robo-machine that I still didn't know how to operate. Thank God for Dallas and Celeste. Both women couldn't make it through a morning without their coffee. I sipped, savoring the tingle of caffeine on my tongue. Black and strong—only way to drink it.

"Where's Feen and Gunner?"

"Gunner's out in the woods still looking for tracks. Started at five this morning. And Feen?" Dallas frowned. "Not sure. His mug's gone, so he's up and around here somewhere."

I glanced into the cupboard where Feen replaced his

mug every morning—a cheap, ceramic black cup that said *'boob man,'* that used to belong to our Dad.

Just then, wearing head-to-toe camo and covered in dirt, Gunner stepped into the kitchen and immediately clicked down the radio. "Like ice picks through my eyes. Who the hell listens to flutes in the mornings?"

"Watch your language," Dallas's narrowed eyes darted over her shoulder. "Wipe your feet, and put in ear plugs."

I filled another cup of coffee, poured in enough sugar to induce a diabetic coma and handed it to him. He nodded and slapped me on the back.

"Find anything from our shooter on the cliff other than the bullet casings?" I asked.

"Nope. Son of a bitch."

"Seems to be the general consensus." I reached around Dallas to grab a slice of bacon and was met with a sharp smack on the wrist.

"Not yet," she said. "Everyone, go wash your hands. We'll start without Feen. Now, Gage, tell me about our new guest. How's she doing?"

The image of Niki up on her tiptoes with that smoldering look in her eyes flashed through my head. I cleared my throat. "She's doing well. Still asleep."

"How do you know this?" A cocked brow accompanied a side eye.

"Just checked the cameras." I lied.

Ax winked, knowing I didn't care to catch the onslaught of questions if Dallas and Gunner knew I'd slept on the porch swing. Hell, I'd been questioning not only that decision, but plenty of things in the last ten minutes. Mainly, how the hell that woman had the ability to throw me off my game so badly the night before.

"Do we need to call Dr. Buckley over today?"

Buckley was Berry Springs' main doctor, still clinging to the old days when house calls were a part of the job. He was a good man and had stitched my brothers and me up more times than I could count.

"No. She's fine."

"She's a tough one." Dallas grabbed a stack of plates from the cabinet.

"What makes you say that?"

"Can see it in her eyes."

Again, I pictured those sultry dark eyes and endless lashes. My stomach dipped. Dammit.

"Sit, boys. Time to eat."

"Ah, just in time." Sliding his phone into his pocket, Wolf walked in the kitchen, wearing his usual uniform of ripped jeans, hoodie, and a baseball cap.

"Morning, Wolf. Cap off. Coffee?"

"Please." He removed his hat. "And Celeste is on her way in, so add a vat to that."

"One cup, black, and a vat, coming up. And a drop cloth." Dallas winked.

A second later, Celeste bustled into the room like a tornado, per usual. We nodded, knowing not to say a single word until she'd had her first sip of coffee. Dallas handed her the *vat,* and she quickly sipped like a drug addict needing a fix.

"Morning, dear." Dallas smiled.

Celeste grunted.

"Uh oh, bad date?"

"If you consider dry BBQ, heavy metal, an ex-girlfriend, and me picking up the tab at the end, yeah, bad date."

I sucked in a breath. Ax released a whistle.

"Seriously, guys..." She launched into one of her infamous rants. "When the hell did men stop being chivalrous?

What happened to romantic dinners, holding the door open for a woman, or helping her out of your stupid jacked-up truck? What happened to *wooing* a woman? Flowers? I mean is there a universal flower shortage I don't know about? Where are the men who give you chocolates? Where are those men?"

"Stuck in the fifties," Wolf muttered, scrolling through his phone.

"Well someone get me a damn time machine then." Sighing, Celeste sank into the chair across from me. "I'm sick of guys thinking I want to gnaw on a pig rib then hit the rodeo simply because I have tattoos and a good arm."

"And a former Marine," I added.

"*And* can outshoot any man in the county, or the Marines, for that matter." Dallas topped off her coffee, already empty. "You're intimidating, Celeste. Men don't know how to respond. Which is why you've got to find one with strength to match." Her eyes drifted to the floor as a moment of silence settled around the table.

Dallas was a walking firecracker and my Dad was probably the only man in the world that could handle it. She'd met her match, and now, was back to square one. Like we all were.

"Anyway," her tone switched and a forced smile crossed her face. "Yesterday sucked. Anniversaries of a loved one's death usually do, which is why I wanted to make you all a big, nice breakfast this morning. Today's a new day. A beautiful day. Let's restart today."

I thought of Niki, and wondered if she was awake, restarting her day. Wondering how that was going for her.

Demanding us to stay in our chairs, Dallas decorated the long, wooden table with a smorgasbord of food. Pancakes—with flax—bacon, sausage, scrambled eggs, warm maple syrup, and a bowl of fresh fruit. We dove in like a bunch of POWs who hadn't seen solid food in months.

Dallas took her seat at the head of the table and added exactly four blueberries and one scoop of eggs onto her plate, then said, "Updates first, then we'll go over the week's schedule. Sound good?"

Nods and grunts around mouthfuls of food.

"Lieutenant Colonel Paranoid Pain-in-my-ass Remy is leaving us today," Ax began the company portion of the update. "His son finally made it in from Australia. Had a long conversation with him yesterday; good guy. He's going to move Remy in with him."

"Good. Family is exactly what that man needs."

"Family and new meds. Which he's on, and promises to continue."

"I'll schedule Opal to get the cabin cleaned up tomorrow, then." Celeste made a note on her phone.

"I think she'll be more than happy to do that. Don't think she's a big fan of Remy." I scooped up a forkful of eggs. "Anyone noticed she seems a bit on edge lately?"

"It's the anniversary of Duke's death," Dallas replied—with a hint of attitude—then changed the subject. "And what about Miss Avery?"

All eyes turned to me.

"Until we find our shooter, she's not safe."

"Agreed," Ax nodded.

"She's going to stay with us until then?"

I swallowed, leaned back. "I'm not sure." The question spread over my brain like a paralyzing virus. Was she going to stay with us until then? Or, was the stubborn, independent Niki Avery going to leave and take matters into her own hands? The thought made my gut clench. Odds were never good for clients who left our services early.

"Well, she's all booked in," Celeste said. "I'll need an idea of a timeframe. And I'm having Dr. Murray pay her a visit this morning, too."

"What?" The fork dropped from my hand. *"No."*

"Why?"

"The woman majored in psychology herself, Celeste. The last thing she's going to want is to be psychoanalyzed today by a psychiatrist."

"Oh, so then, she doesn't need to talk about what happened?" Celeste snapped back with an attitude and sarcasm as thick as the maple syrup she'd poured on her mile-high stack of pancakes.

"Not saying that," I snapped back. "Shit, drink your coffee, C-note."

"I'm just saying, *Gage,* the woman is a sexual assault victim—"

"No, she's not. The guy never touched her that way. It never got that far." The heat started rising up my neck. Damn temper.

"Doesn't make a difference, you blockhead. She got her ass kicked, then killed a guy who had every intention of assaulting her. Not everyone is trained for that, Gage. Even we are ordered to see a head doctor after we kill someone. A civilian? No, there's no way in hell you can't convince me that Niki Avery doesn't need to talk to some-one. A trained professional." She focused on me, her eyes narrowed with warning—and I noticed everyone else was giving me the same look, too. She continued. "Hell, Gage, that woman is not thinking straight right now. She needs to be met with by a professional and then given some time to work things out on her own. She certainly doesn't need anything *else* on her emotional plate right now." She paused for emphasis, her eyes boring into me. "Right now, Niki Avery is a walking time bomb of bad decisions."

The last sentence hit me like a brick wall, flashing with a picture of her lips against mine.

Bad decisions...

15

GAGE

*W*ith a full stomach and attitude to match, I was the first to leave the breakfast table. The conversation about Niki was as subtle as a mule kick to the face.

Don't get involved with that girl.

The message was clear.

Do *not* have sex with Niki Avery.

Got it.

You see, when I was younger, I was the kid that did exactly what he was told *not* to do. Call it defiance, call it a punk-ass brat, but restrictions and I didn't mix. Never did. Thing was, half the stuff I was told not to do, I wouldn't have even considered if not for the caution sign wrapped around it.

Thing was, the more you told me to stay away from something, the more I decided I wanted to try it.

Little did Celeste and my family know, the constant attention the situation was getting, the constant don't-touch-her reminders only made it worse. A perfect storm of you-want-what-you-can't-have *and* save-the-damsel-in-distress. It was like someone putting a T-bone in front of a rabid dog.

And I was hungry... not for any kind of meat, I'd noticed, I was hungry only for my client in Cabin 1.

That threw me off.

As I took my plate to the sink, I wondered—was that all it was?

Did I only want Niki because I couldn't have her?

I quickly decided that whatever feelings I was getting for Niki better be nothing deeper than that because if I fucked up—*if I fucked Niki*—I'd be out of a job or banished from personal security, at the very least.

Frustrated—and worse, doubting myself—I haphazardly wiped the plate, set it in the dishwasher and considered a drive to Frank's Bar for a few Bloody Marys and a roll in the hay with whichever bartender was on call. A smooth drink and smoother woman was exactly what I needed to cool my irritation—and my thoughts about Niki. A good lay was exactly what I needed.

First, though, I needed to figure out why the hell my oldest brother, Feen, was MIA.

I left the chatter behind, a heated debate about women paying for dinners, and jogged up the staircase to the second floor. After checking for Feen in his room, I checked the gym, the garage, then the shooting range via the security cameras. No Phoenix. I checked the back deck—sometimes Feen would drink his morning coffee outside—then I headed back inside. Frowning, I searched the main level, unease beginning to mix with the pancakes in my stomach.

Feen had been *off* over the last forty-eight hours, then again, we all were. Death anniversaries were never fun, especially when it belonged to your dad. The only difference was that Gunner, Ax, and I drew strength from each other, each rather having a prostate exam than show pain. It's how we dealt with it. Feen, on the other hand, had been wound tighter than a two dollar watch.

Something was up with the guy and I needed to find out what that was.

Back upstairs, I made my way down the east hallway and stopped at the door that had remained closed for the last year—only entered by Opal, our housekeeper, and that was simply to dust around the things we'd asked her not to touch. None of us went into that room, ever... except for Phoenix, apparently.

I turned the brass knob and pushed open the thick, wooden door.

Dad.

I could smell him, the scent of his spicy cologne hung in the air like a memory still clinging onto the present. My stomach sank.

God, I missed him.

Feen sat behind our father's desk, everything in his office in the exact position it had been on the day he died. The same monogrammed pen laying vertically on personalized stationary. The same Newton's Cradle pendulum balls that no longer swung. The same family picture, slowly fading in the sunlight.

Books lined the walls, all dark cherry oak, file cabinets, and in the center of the room, a multi-computer set up that looked more like a command center for a warship, which, some might say was fitting for the kind of work my Dad did. A command center that was now buzzing with life, with Feen behind the controls.

I quickly closed the door behind me with a glance over my shoulder.

"What the hell are you doing, brother?" I crossed the

authentic Chinese rug, concern brewing like a green batch of beer.

No response.

"Feen."

Just noticing me, Feen looked up and leaned back in our dad's massive leather chair. He ran his fingers through his mussed, greasy hair. His eyes were shaded, heavy with bags that added ten years to his age. His skin was pale, pasty even. He looked like shit.

My instinct went to alert. "What's wrong with you?"

In a mindless tick, Feen started shaking his head side to side. Like a damn mental patient. My frown deepened as I walked around the desk and zeroed in on the computer screen where multiple reports and spreadsheets covered the monitors. Below, a piece of notebook paper with Feen's scribbled writing all over it.

"I repeat. What the hell is wrong with you?"

An exasperated exhale, then, "Dad was into something, Gage." His voice was weak and scratchy as if he'd been to a rager the night before.

I held up a hand. "No, hang on. Are *you* okay?"

Feen's eyes skirted around the desk, for what I wasn't sure. My instincts were at five-alarm stage now. I turned, quickly walked into the bathroom, grabbed a rinsing cup and filled it with cold water. My brother chugged it, then took a deep breath.

"Better?"

"Yeah. Thanks."

"Now. Go. What's going on?"

"Dad was researching something... something big before he died. I've... I've been filtering through shit since yesterday morning."

"Yesterday morning? Why didn't you tell us?"

"Tell you what?" Attitude flashed in his eyes, which, honestly, made me feel better. It was life in him, and at that moment, that's what I needed to see. He continued, "That I was finally going to take action on my hunch that Dad didn't actually die of a heart attack? That he was murdered? *Please.* Get out of here with that."

He had a point. Ax, Gunner, and I—and Dallas for that matter—would have done everything we could to keep him from exploring a conspiracy theory we'd all been forced to put to bed a year earlier. It wasn't healthy. *Obviously,* it wasn't healthy. Feen looked like he'd caught a rabid case of food poisoning.

"Okay, fine." I shook my head and held up my hands to surrender. "What have you found?"

"Okay..." He spoke quickly, the words pouring out in a hyped up, jittery run-on sentence. "So you know the NSA is responsible for monitoring and analyzing foreign and domestic data to provide intelligence to the military..."

"Right."

"You also know that Dad specialized in cryptology—in writing and analyzing code. He was smart as shit."

"Yeah, Ax is the only one who got that gene."

Feen snorted. "Anyway, I found some encrypted files buried deep in Dad's hard drive—"

"Encrypted?"

"Yeah."

My eyes narrowed. "We just agreed that Ax is the only smart one in the family, so how the hell did you find these—and then actually get into them?"

No answer.

"Feen..."

He looked up at me with a grim expression. "Wolf helped."

"*Wolf?*"

"Yeah..."

"You had our employee help you with something behind your brothers' backs? Something you shouldn't even be doing in the first place?"

Feen surged to his feet—startling the shit out of me—sending the chair tumbling backward and me taking a step back, and thankful that I wouldn't need to grab a new pair of shorts on the way out.

"Someone *had* to do this, Gage!" His voice boomed through the silent room. Rage, the color of blood, spilled from his eyes. The guy was literally shaking.

He was a total, complete nut job.

This had to stop.

I stepped forward, toe to toe, jaw clenched. "Cool it, Phoenix."

My heartbeat started to pick up as he stared down at me, fingers beginning to tingle like they used to the moment before Feen and I would pummel each other for whatever argument we'd gotten into. But that was decades ago...

The flare of his nostrils eased and he finally stepped back. I chocked that up to exhaustion. Ol' badass Feen had never backed down from a fight. *Ever.*

Yeah, *this guy* was on the brink of a mental breakdown.

"Sit." I told him. "And keep your voice down unless you want the entire family coming up here. Jesus, Feen, Dallas would *flip out* if she knew what you were doing."

He sat as he'd been told—shocking me—and scrubbed his hands over his face, taking a deep breath. It was that moment that I realized he didn't sit because I demanded it, he sat in concession because he needed something from me. He needed my help, and he knew it.

I crossed my arms over my chest, more intrigued than

ever, and angled behind him, peering at the computer screen.

"As I was saying," he started again. "I've been going through these encrypted files..."

"Hang on. Why? Dad probably had thousands of encrypted files on his computer, right? Why'd you go through these in particular?"

"Because, Gage, these were on his *personal* computer. Not his work computer."

My eyebrows raised.

"What I've gathered is that Dad was researching *off the books*. Investigating something personally. Something big. And guess when the time stamp is for the first file he pulled?"

"Don't fucking tell me..."

"Two days before he died."

I blew out a breath and dragged my fingers through my hair. *Christ.* "Do we know what he was researching?"

After a few clicks, Feen pulled up a black and white photo of a man, mid-sixties, draped in military garb and brandishing an AK-15.

"You recognize this guy?"

I shook my head, running through the most wanted list I used to know by heart.

"That's Andrei Sokolov, with the FSB."

"The Russian secret service?"

"Yep. He was the director over military counterintelligence."

"Was?"

"Yep. Assassinated a few weeks before Dad died. According to these restricted files, Sokolov caught a bullet in the brain one night while sleeping in his bed... under heavy security, I might add. No one knows how someone snuck into his home, or more importantly, why he was killed. News spun it that—get this—he died of a heart attack."

"How did Dad get these files?"

Feen shrugged. "I'm sure he pulled it directly from one of our government's hacking groups that no one knows about. Dad had full security clearance."

"Okay, so what does this Sokolov cat have to do with making you think Dad's death was no accident?"

"Well, Dad was researching Sokolov's assassination extensively, along with this..." he clicked a few more keys, bringing up a black screen with an eye-crossing amount of tiny-ass code running across it. "...this code, or key, I should say. Dad was researching something called QKD, or quantum cryptography."

"What the hell is quantum cryptography?"

"According to Wolf, it's basically a way to communicate through satellites. It's a way to send a password key that's used to decrypt some form of communication." He grabbed a stack of papers, spilling the water I'd gotten for him. After wiping up the mess, he pointed to a bunch of hand-written notes across various geographic print-outs. "Look here, this key correlates to a specific satellite."

My brows squeezed together to ward off an impending headache. "One of *our* satellites?"

"Yep. And according to Dad's notes here, Dad believed the key was *embedded* into our satellite system."

"Embedded as in... *secretly* embedded?"

"Exactly. This key was used to decrypt emails between two people, a group of people, whatever. It's almost completely untraceable. But here's the deal." Feen pulled up another image of the code, highlighted in various rows. In the upper corner was a date, handwritten and circled several times. "That's Dad's writing. It's the date the code was discovered. Guess when that date is?"

"Let me guess... the date Sokolov was assassinated."

"Exactly." Feen smiled, leaned back and blew out a breath like he'd just aced his SAT. Something none of us, aside from Ax—and Wolf, for that matter—had ever done.

Squinting, I leaned forward, scanning each screen. "So you're saying that a few days before Dad died, he was researching a secret code embedded into one of our satellites, and believes this code correlates to the assassination of Russia's Director of Military Counterintelligence of the FSB."

"Doesn't just correlate, Gage, whoever killed Sokolov was *secretly* sending password keys to decrypt confidential communication, through our satellites. Meaning someone here, in the US, was involved. *And* two days after Dad discovers this hidden code, he dies of a massive heart attack."

A ball formed in the pit of my stomach. "Jesus, Feen."

"I know."

A moment slid by.

"Gage."

Feen's tone sent a chill up my spine. I shifted my gaze from the computer to him.

"That's not all." He scrolled down to show the backside of the code printout that had been scanned to Dad's account. "Look..."

I leaned in. Underlined and circled several times in red ink, were two words scribbled across the paper in our dad's writing.

Knight Fox

I looked at Feen, my insides twisting. "Who's Knight Fox?"

"No idea."

Holy. Shit. My stomach clenched knowing that my brother had just ripped off the top of Pandora's box.

"I thought about asking Dad's buddies at the NSA, but, frankly, Gage, how do we know that someone from the government didn't secretly assassinate Sokolov?" He glanced over his shoulder. "And maybe that person killed Dad. I don't think we can trust anyone right now."

"Can you trace the embedded code? See where it came from, or where it originated from?"

"According to Wolf, that's nearly impossible. He's going to work on it, though."

"You need to bring Ax in on this."

Feen nodded, "I know. I wanted to keep it quiet from you guys until I got something solid. Black and white facts that we could act on. We don't have that yet... but we have a name."

"The Knight Fox," I whispered under my breath.

Silent, we stared at the screen, together, each knowing, understanding, that this information just changed the course of our family's future.

"I'm going to find out who he is. Somewhere in these files, there's clues, links to it all. The Knight Fox is the link to figuring out why Dad was murdered."

"Or, the Knight Fox is the man who murdered him." *Unbelievable.* In a daze of information, I straightened and crossed the room to the window.

I'd just walked directly into my own nightmare. The thought that someone had targeted my dad, my family, was almost too much to bare. Phoenix had been right all along —Dad's death wasn't an accident.

Dad had been murdered.

Maybe I knew. Maybe deep in my gut I knew that, too. Maybe that was why I'd been drinking and screwing my way through the last year.

As I looked down at the land my Dad had worked so hard for, I only knew one thing for certain.

The Knight Fox better fucking run.

16

NIKI

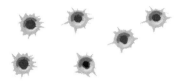

*B*linking, I pulled away from my laptop, where I'd spent the entire afternoon filtering through not only Mickey Greco's case files, but old files as well, looking for anything that could lead me to my attacker. My current stalker. I had a notebook full of incoherent notes, names, dates, a few doodles of a tornado, block letters, flowers... and *GS* scribbled more times than I cared to admit. At least I hadn't doodled *NS* with a heart around it, like some tragically love-stricken eighth grader.

I grabbed the beer I'd been sipping on for the last hour and swigged the rest.

I needed a break.

Leaning back against the couch, my gaze settled on the sweeping windows where the sun was beginning to set. Bright orange, yellow, and fuchsia painted the sky, shooting through the woods like slanted fire. But the view that pulled me the most were the glimpses of the main house through the trees.

Gage.

I picked my red leaf and twirled it around in my fingers.

Gage.

Yes, I needed a break, and I knew exactly where to go.

I carefully set the leaf down, stood, and paused to grab my phone. Remembering that I didn't have one was like the sugar-free icing on top of a raw, vegan carrot cake.

Not good.

Just like the day I'd just had.

So, instead, I grabbed my *SOS* necklace and security remote and paused in front of the mirror. I grimaced at the knot below my eye, now a hundred different shades of purple. The swelling had gone down, though—*yee-haw*. In an attempt to refresh myself, I finger-combed my hair, my nails catching on the curls that had formed at the bottom from going to bed with wet hair the night before. Resigning to the disheveled look, I glanced down at my clothes, a white cashmere sweater with skinny jeans, courtesy of Celeste. After a quick dab of lip gloss to distract from the shiner below my eye, I shrugged and pushed out the back door of Cabin 1.

Taking a deep breath, I inhaled the fresh, autumn air, and felt the tension release from my shoulders. The knots from the evening before had been compounded by a surprise visit that morning by a very pushy psychiatrist named Dr. Murray. Well, pushy might be a stretch but when I'd made it evident to the doctor that I had zero interest in replaying the attack for the hundredth time, she'd proceeded to do exactly what I would have done—ask probing personal questions thinly veiled to lead to an emotional breakthrough. Or, breakdown.

Well, sweetheart, I'd already broken down. And break through? I wanted to break Gage's face for scheduling the little appointment to begin with. Although... it'd be difficult to break the man's face who'd slept on my deck to ensure no one else dropped off their heads, or their bullets into my body.

It would be difficult to break the man's face who'd captivated my every thought since the moment he'd kissed me.

It had been a sleepless night with visions of Gage Steele running through my mind, the man who'd rescued me from the woods, saved my life, and kissed me with more passion than I'd ever felt before.

There was a heat between us.

Raw.

Unprecedented.

Volatile.

Magic.

Like fire and gasoline.

I reminded myself, though, of course there was passion. Gage was a walking bottle of testosterone, unable to control, conceal, or hide the fire that so evidently raged inside him. A scorching passion that could only be dulled by booze and women. The ultimate alpha male—controlling, demanding, and quick to label anything he wanted as his own.

He wanted me. I could feel it in his touch, see it in his eyes.

He wanted me, and I needed to be careful.

Men like Gage didn't settle down. With one woman, at least. Men like Gage could never be tamed.

Men like Gage had heartbreaker written all over their gorgeous, ruggedly handsome faces.

No, I didn't date men like Gage... no matter how many butterflies he gave me.

I'd repeated that mantra throughout the day.

After my appointment with the head doctor, Gunner had dropped off my laptop, moments before I'd met with both Lieutenant Colson and Officer Haddix for the third time in the last twenty-four hours to answer another onslaught of questions, and to discuss my theory that the infamous Mickey Greco was somehow involved. It became apparent that BSPD and the Steele brothers were a tight knit group, and that they'd been in communication since the attack and shooting. It was another example of how far the Steele family reached.

That meeting ended with the officers informing me it would be forty-eight more hours until my Jeep was released, and they strongly recommended that I continue my stay at Steele B&B until advancements were made in the case. I responded by asking how close they were to finding my attacker-turned-gunman, to which they responded with glances at their shoes.

After *that* discouraging meeting, that's when I took matters into my own hands and dove into my case files. My only break was to write a carefully worded email to my boss, informing him of the "incident", where I was, and that I'd work remotely when I could.

The afternoon had quickly faded to dusk and, at that point, I had all the pent up energy and anger of a caged tiger. I felt like I was about to internally combust.

I needed space, air, time to breathe. If the son of a bitch was still looking for me with his rifle and poor aim, then so be it. Because truth be told, at that point, I didn't give a damn.

Truth be told, I knew I was safe on the grounds of the compound, and probably nowhere else.

Dammit. Damn them for having me under their thumbs.

I wiped a pile of dead leaves from the seat of my covered golf cart—approved by Steele Shadows Security, apparently —then headed down the manicured trail through the woods.

The trees were at their autumn peak, glittering in the golden rays of dusk. Endless rows of oaks, maples, and pines fading into the mountains. Colorful leaves swirled around me with the breeze, a raining color of yellow and orange. It was breathtakingly beautiful and I found myself picturing Gage, as a child, running through those woods playing cops and robbers.

No doubt Gage was the robber.

I came to a fork in the trail, one that led to the main house, the other somewhere down the hill, to the back yard.

I decided on taking the scenic route.

I took my time descending down the trail, experiencing the first moments of the closest thing to relaxation I'd felt. The stillness, serenity, peacefulness of the woods around me... until I heard—

"Aw, *fuck* you, you cheap-shodding son of a bitch!"

I recognized the voice, which only meant it was one of the Steele brothers because they all sounded the same. I veered off the trail, following the sound of rock and roll music, accompanied by thuds, slaps, and pops. My brow cocked, my imagination running wild with what I was about to drive up on.

An orgy perhaps?

No telling with those guys.

The woods opened up to a sprawling back yard, complete with an infinity pool speckled with verandas and beer cans. An outdoor kitchen, seating area, and multiple flat-screens hugged the stone walls. A tennis court, basketball court... and then there was Gage and a beast of a man, colored in mean-looking tattoos, engaged in some sort of mixed martial arts hand-to-hand combat crap. They were inside a UFC-style fighting cage... Both wearing nothing but spandex shorts. Gage's, bright red, of course. Grinning, I parked under a tree and got out, watching the violent attack unfold in front of me.

The dark-haired tattoo-guy had Gage by a few inches, but matched in shredded muscle and brute force. A spit-laden mouth piece flew across the mat as tattoo-man popped Gage in the mouth, to which Gage responded with a devastating roundhouse kick to tattoo's kidneys. Then, he barreled into the guy, sending them both into the air and slamming onto the mat.

"You're losing it, Jagg." Gage muttered through an evil grin, and I realized tattoo-man must be the detective I'd heard about earlier.

Fists flew, legs kicked, grunts, spits, curse words as I walked up to the cage. I watched Gage, the fluidity of his movements, the confidence in his nimble, quick steps. No thinking, no hesitating, just deadly force, *boom, boom, boom,* one hit after another. The rawness of it, the intensity—the manliness—of it had me licking my lips like a schoolgirl watching the quarterback practice on the field. God, he was gorgeous, a tanned, ripped body so toned it belonged on the cover of a men's fitness magazine. A few nasty scars slashed his back reminding me of his past life in the Marines. Gage Steele had spent his whole life fighting.

Dominating. Exactly like he was then.

My gaze was pulled to the bulge between his legs and, I swear to God, my heart stopped beating for two seconds. Heat rose to my cheeks as I cleared my throat and looked away. Gage Steele was the sexiest man I'd ever laid eyes on.

Like a magnet, I watched him.

He shifted underneath Jagg, his face catching a beam of light. Our eyes met, and the world stopped. He froze, and my heart did the opposite, slipping in my chest as he stared back at me.

Then, he was pinned to the mat... *One. Two. Three.*

Game over.

Victorious now, and straddled on top of Gage, Jagg grinned at me, then leaned down and whispered something in Gage's ear. I couldn't make out Gage's response but heard several f-bombs and a threat that I was pretty sure would land him in a padded room under a federal prison.

Jagg laughed and released him. Gage pushed off the mat, locked eyes with me and after a quick drink, he began crossing the lawn in nothing but his underwear.

Sweat dripped down his face, his body, the band of his spandex saturated. I felt my body come to life, a tingle below, a zing of sexual awakening, as if I needed any reminder that this man was capable of bringing a woman to her knees with nothing more than one of those cocky grins. He stared at me, as if daring me to look away. He crossed the grass with a swagger, a twinkle in his eye and—God help me —a small curve of his lips as he drew closer. He'd either forgotten that he was wearing nothing more than a strap of spandex, or didn't care... or, perhaps, Gage knew exactly what he looked like, and what he was doing... what he was doing *to me.*

Damn the confidence. It got me every time.

I reminded myself to get a grip and, in an attempt to act aloof, I looked away and focused on Jagg, toweling off in the ring.

He was hot, too, after all.

"Well, hey there." Gage said immediately when my eyes left him, demanding my attention back on him. He stopped in front of me, perfectly blocking my view of Jagg.

Jealous? Interesting.

"Hey," I smiled, my heart a little pitter patter.

He flicked my hair, a flirty gesture. "I like it down."

"Well your approval means everything to me."

"I bet it does," he grinned and I noticed several welts forming on his face, scratches down his arms. Damn, he and his buddies went hard. He didn't seem to notice, or care, that he looked like he'd been in a street fight. I assumed the latter.

"It's good to see you." He shifted closer to me, teasing me, reminding me of the kiss we'd shared. Letting me know that he wanted it again. That was Gage—as subtle as an explosion.

"You know, I like that necklace on you." He fingered the security pendant around my neck. The mere touch of his fingertips sent goosebumps over my skin.

I shifted my weight to my heels reminding myself I couldn't jump him right there, and looked behind him. "Nice set up back here."

Still holding the necklace, and me by the neck, he ignored the compliment.

"How was your day?" He asked.

"Why don't you ask Dr. Murray?" My attitude thick.

"Ah, you enjoyed it then." He smirked.

"As much as you enjoyed getting pinned by your buddy just then."

"Hey, that was *your* fault." The pendant dropped from his hands, sending a cool draft against my heated skin.

I crossed my arms over my chest, drawing his gaze like a laser beam. "I thought Marines are trained not to get distracted."

"Doesn't include uptight, stubborn, brown-haired lawyers with lips that could..." he sucked in a breath, "wanna go back to the cabin?" He shifted his weight back and forth with a twinkle in his eye.

My lip curved, watching him, all hyped up on adrenaline

from a fight, and I was on the receiving end of that pent up energy. It was like he couldn't control himself, or again, was simply enjoying throwing me off my game.

"Maybe later," I said, turning him down. As the words came out of my mouth, I realized that deep down, I meant it.

"I'll take that as a promise." He winked. "Now, what's got you out and about? Is everything okay in your cabin?"

"Do most of your clients stay cooped up in their cabins the whole time they're here?"

"Yes."

"Well, I'm not most of your clients then, I guess."

"No, you're definitely not. Most of my clients don't kiss me."

"Most?"

He laughed. Then, his face sombered as if remembering something. "You should keep your next appointment with Dr. Murray."

"Why?"

"She's good at what she does."

"That's not why you want me to keep the appointment. Why, Gage?"

He stepped back, the adrenaline from the fight fading from him. "Just want to make sure you're... thinking straight."

"Hey buddy, *you* kissed *me*. Remember?"

"Then you kissed me."

"So, what?" I fisted my hands on my hips. "You think I can't control my impulses simply because I had a traumatic experience?"

"Yes."

My eyebrows shot up. I laughed a humorless laugh and turned away. "Well, I'm glad we got that out of the way. *Jesus,* Gage. Have a nice day."

"Dammit," he growled behind me. "Wait, Niki..."

Just then a loud whistle cut through the air. We turned to see Celeste waving from one of the hundred balconies on the house.

Gage shaded his eyes from the setting sun. "What?" He snapped.

"You have a visitor. Out front."

"Get what they want and send them away."

Celeste's gaze flickered to me. "Actually the visitor came to see Niki."

Gage turned to me, all pissed and frowning in one expression.

I blinked. A visitor? For me?

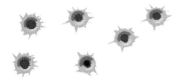

 y mind was spinning trying to think of who would visit me, who knew I was there beside my boss? I followed Gage up the back yard, past the pool, and into the house. We passed two housekeepers, one who didn't make eye contact. I assumed it was because Gage was striding through the house half-naked... and I wondered if she'd seen him actually naked. For some reason, I'd bet my life on it. The other locked onto me like a bird with its prey, eyeing me from behind red-rimmed glasses and long, grey dreadlocks. Unwelcomed; got it.

He guided me through the kitchen, then led me to the side door.

"Wait... Gage."

"What?"

"Uhhh..." I nodded to his groin. "Aren't you going to put some clothes on?"

He frowned, confused by this request.

"Seriously, Gage."

"Does it make you uncomfortable, Niki? Whoever's out there can't handle it?"

"It's not the first time I've seen a guy in his underwear, Gage, but whoever is here to see me might notice that you're half naked. Put on some shorts, at least."

A car door slammed outside and Gage glanced out the window. He shot me a look, then snorted and muttered, "Oh, *hell* no."

Gage stormed out the door and strode outside in his cherry-red spandex like the stubborn pain in the ass he was. I followed him and stopped cold, gaping at my ex-boyfriend standing in front of his sparkling new F-150.

Paul Taylor.

Paul freaking Taylor.

Paul wasn't looking at me though, nope, he was locked onto the naked man bowed up like a Rottweiler bee-lining it to him across the driveway. Gage was rigid, tense, totally amped up. I didn't understand what he was so pissed about. Surely their clients got visitors.

I shook myself from my shocked stupor and walked across the driveway.

"Who are you?" Gage demanded.

Christ, what the hell was his problem? I jogged to catch up with him.

"His name is Paul—"

Paul cut me off, chest puffed to meet Gage's. "Paul Taylor." His eyes narrowed to slits. "Niki's boyfriend."

"*Ex*-boyfriend," I quickly corrected, feeling like I'd stepped into the twilight zone, or some cheesy eighties flick.

Gage's fingers flexed at his side and then it hit me—he wasn't pissed, he was *jealous.* I inwardly laughed. It shouldn't have surprised me. Gage Steele couldn't control his emotions. Throwing a jealous temper tantrum fit right in with the irrational behavior I'd seen so far.

Gage shifted his weight, angling in front of me.

Not *just* jealous...

Protective.

Possessive.

Extremely possessive.

And it was escalating.

I shifted my attention to Gage, and spoke to him with kid gloves. "Can Paul and I have a moment, please?"

With his eyes locked on my former boyfriend, he grabbed my hand, forcefully, and replied, "That's not how it works here, sweetheart."

"Don't call her sweetheart."

My hand was dropped and Gage stepped forward, the veins bulging in his neck. I grabbed his forearm.

"Hey." My heart was speeding like a racehorse. I kept my voice low, level, calm. "Give us a minute. *Please.*" I tugged at his arm when he didn't look at me. I looked back and forth between both men, my former boyfriend with his blonde, perfectly coifed hair, long, lean tall body, falling only an inch or two shorter than the hot-headed body-builder roughneck in front of him.

Gage would have Paul out cold in under five seconds.

"Please," I said again. "Give us a sec."

Gage finally turned to me, glowering. A solid ten seconds stretched out as I waited for him to grace us with his decision. Finally, he flashed Paul a warning glance, then stepped to the side, arms crossed over his chest watching us like a snarling guard dog.

I tried to pretend he was gone.

"What are you doing here?" I couldn't hide the shock, the annoyance in my voice.

"I heard what happened, Niki, *shit,* are you okay?" Paul focused on my bruised eye.

"Yes, I'm fine. Again, what are you doing here?"

"I wanted to check on you. Make sure you were okay."

"I'm fine. Thank you." Still baffled, I shook my head. "How'd you hear about everything?"

"Cami told me."

Cami—the receptionist at my law office. Apparently, my boss had told her, not realizing she was one of the biggest gossips in town.

"I don't think many other people know, though. And I won't tell anyone." He flickered a glance over my shoulder then stepped forward, closing the inches between us. He was taunting Gage. I didn't like it. For whatever reason, I didn't like it.

"Do you need anything, at all?"

"No, I'm fine. Thank you."

He reached forward to touch my arm but was stopped when a foam football came hurling through the air and slammed into his temple.

"What the *hell,* man?" Paul pushed past me, the anger in his eyes now matching my guard dog's. "What the *fuck?*"

"Oops." Gage popped his knuckles.

That didn't deter Paul as he stomped up to him, red-faced and ready to fight.

A winked grin crossed Gage's face. His fingers curled into fists.

The football returned, this time from the opposite direction, and landed perfectly in-between the impending fist fight. Paul and I both turned to see Ax, striding across the driveway, as Gunner pushed out the front door.

All eyes on Paul.

Daring him to make a move.

Paul looked at me, his face flushed with adrenaline, then back at the massive men descending upon him, knowing that he was screwed. Visibly frustrated, he picked up the football and hurled it into the woods.

No one even flinched.

"How can I help ya, buddy?" Ax asked, condescending with a touch of sarcasm.

Gunner positioned himself behind Gage, no doubt to hold him back in case he snapped. One more second, and I was sure he would have. Gunner handed him a pair of shorts, which Gage responded to by throwing them on the ground like a child.

The Steele brothers. Always there for each other. Every second, of every day. It was remarkable to watch. Each having their unsaid role to diffuse the situation.

It was as if they'd done it a hundred times, and I wondered... was Gage this possessive with all his female clients?

Their stepmother, Dallas, walked out, into the covered entryway, arms crossed over her chest. Her gaze shifted from man to man, disapproval narrowing her eyes.

Paul looked at the Steele army encircling him, and recoiled. "I came out here to check on Niki... I can see she's in good hands, apparently." He spat on the ground.

"Spit again and you'll be licking it up between two broken teeth, buddy. Now, if there's nothing else..." Ax motioned to Paul's truck.

One more look in my direction, and another at Gage, then Paul turned, jumped in his truck and disappeared down the driveway.

Ax nodded at Gage, who nodded back, then the Steele brothers and their stepmother descended into the shadows and went back to whatever they were doing before they saved their brother from getting slapped with an assault charge.

I spun on my heel and stomped up to Gage, now wearing a pair of jogging shorts over his spandex. Good. I didn't need that distraction.

"What the *hell* is your problem, Gage?"

"What the hell is yours? Sending your little boyfriends over here to check on you? Think I can't do my job?"

"You're *unbelievable,* you know that?" I breezed past him and started down the hill to my golf cart.

"Funny choice of words coming from you, Niki Avery."

My eyes popped with shock—no, rage. I spun around. "How *dare* you."

"Hey man, just stating the facts."

"I am *not* a liar. I am *not* my father."

"Apple usually doesn't fall too far from the tree."

"This apple does. And you should know." I turned and started speed-walking down the hill, him hot on my heels.

"Now, what the hell is *that* supposed to mean?"

"Oh give me a break. You know exactly what it means." I dropped into the golf cart, my foot fumbling to release the brake.

"Scoot over." He snarled.

My mouth dropped. The gall of this guy.

"I said scoot over. I have the keys. Scoot over."

I heaved out a breath and scooted over. Dammit.

"Go on... Tell me more of what you think of me, Niki. Didn't have enough of a go at me last night?" He jerked the wheel and we took off into the woods. The sun had disappeared below the mountains, twilight darkening the woods —fitting for the firestorm of energy between us.

I went in like a son of a bitch.

"You and your brothers, you're all the same. Bad apples. You're nothing but a cocky playboy with the emotional capacity of a five year old. You're a drunk who can't control your impulses, or articulate your feelings to save your life. You're a ladies' man, the worst kind, who look at women as flashy toys, shiny objects, instead of worthy opponents."

I grabbed the side as he took a corner much too quickly. I didn't dare look at him, hell, I could feel his rage radiating from where I was sitting. We hit a bump, I came out of my seat.

"Slow *down, Gage."*

He didn't, of course, just kept going until finally, he skidded to a stop in front of Cabin 1.

His neck snapped to me. "When was the last time you were with him?"

"What?"

"You know exactly what I'm asking."

"That is none of your business."

"It is my business. I need to know."

I shook my head and snorted, then stared into the woods for a few seconds before I responded. "Paul and I dated for two months, and broke up a few weeks ago. He's an attorney; that's how we met. He helped me through a lot of my cases, to be honest. Anyway, we didn't work out so I broke up with him and that was that."

"Only two months?"

"Yeah, and *barely* dated, even. Maybe five dates."

His jaw twitched. "Ended a few weeks ago?"

"*Yes.*" I snapped.

"Have you seen him since?"

"No, not that that's any of your business. And for the freaking record, we didn't even sleep together. There. There's the answer to the question you don't even have the balls to ask directly." I could literally feel my hands shaking. I got out of the cart, then turned, braced my palms on the top and leaned down, glaring. "And I want to make one thing clear. I believe in monogamy. I'm a one man woman, Gage, and I expect the same in return. Men like you don't change. Men like you can't be tamed, so let's forget about the kiss last night. And keep your fucking hands off me." I pushed off the top and stomped onto the porch.

I didn't hear him, didn't see him, but I felt him right behind me as I stopped at the front door.

"Turn around."

I didn't move.

"Turn around."

Folding my arms over my chest, I turned.

He stared down at me, all storm, all anger... all desperation.

"Is that really what you think of me?"

I lifted my chin. "It is."

He nodded, looking me over from head to toe, his mind racing. Finally, he said, "Do you think that's who I want to be, Niki? My life took a nose dive when my dad died. I miss the military like I'd miss my right arm. We all do. But we did what we had to do, and we're all adjusting. In different ways. My oldest brother, Phoenix..." Gage blew out a breath, shaking his head. "... believes our dad was murdered, and between you and me, I'm beginning to think it, too. How's that for a revelation? So yeah, I'm a bit on edge tonight. Yeah, I've drunk too much since I've been back, and yeah, I've screwed a lot of women, Niki..." He reached up and placed his palms against the door, on either side of my head. Closing me in, trapping me... making my heart skip a beat.

"Maybe it's because I've never met a woman who challenged me." He leaned closer, his voice low. My heartbeat tripled in an instant.

"I've never met a woman who made my head spin like a top in a hurricane. Who makes me act like a crazed jealous lunatic because I can't bear the thought of her being with anyone else. Who I'd step in front of a fucking bullet for." He leaned inches from my lips.

I was all but gasping for air.

"You, Niki Avery," he whispered. "Are a worthy opponent."

18

NIKI

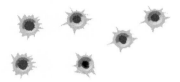

*H*is lips met mine with a force, a hunger, like a tidal wave, explosive, disintegrating my anger, fear, all of my thoughts and commanding submission. Like being tossed around on the bottom of the ocean, I was completely lost in his kiss, not knowing right from left, up from down, only knowing that I wanted this man.

At that moment, nothing else mattered.

My hand fumbled with the doorknob as his tongue swirled around mine, his hard body pressed against mine. My hand was swatted away, and while keeping his mouth and focus on me, he entered the security code.

Click—the door flew open, taking our bodies with it. I stumbled backward unable to withstand the force of the man bearing down on me like his next breath was his last.

He backed me up, my hip swiping an end table, sending it teetering and clamoring on the floor. I trusted him, blindly, as he pushed me backward across the dark cabin, and into the bedroom, dark as night. I was spun around like a rag doll and slammed against the wall, pinned underneath him.

A painting fell to the floor.

"Jesus, Niki." He murmured between kisses as he grabbed a fist full of my hair in his palm.

My heart felt like a jackhammer in my chest. I closed my eyes submitting myself to the moment. To the rush.

He lightly pulled my hair, tipping my chin up, exposing my neck to him.

A vampire about to devour its prey.

My eyes fluttered open, focusing on the blue glow of twilight outside.

Fitting.

My scalp tingled as he gripped harder, squeezing the strands of my hair like he was clinging onto life. Burying himself in my neck, he licked, kissed, nipped. Goosebumps flew over my skin from the heat of his breath, his tongue trailing down my jugular.

Primal.

He pressed himself into my hip, pinning my entire body. My hair in his hand, my neck beneath his lips, my hips under his erection.

My body at his mercy.

I'd had sex before, but had never—*ever*—felt an animal-istic passion as I did right then. It was an uncontrollable urge, a want, a need to feel him inside me. For him to *take me.* Like my body was screaming out for him.

It was *him.*

It was Gage Steele.

I dragged my fingernails over the taught skin of his tanned back. A groan escaped his lips as he pressed harder into me, grinding, his fingers combing through my hair.

I was gripped at the biceps, lifted, swirled around and backed up to the bed.

He stopped in front of me, his massive chest rising and

falling heavily. Wide shoulders, round pecs, a scarred six-pack leading down to a bulge in his shorts that would make even the most seasoned hooker blush. With eyes wild with fiery passion, he looked me over, every inch of my skin tingling under his gaze.

Keeping his eyes on me, he backed up and clicked on the bathroom light. A dim golden light pooled into the dark room, barely illuminating the space.

"Off," he demanded, nodding to my sweater.

I stared back, slowly gripping the bottom of the cashmere, the fabric silk sweeping against my skin as I slowly took it off.

His jaw clenched.

I continued my erotic strip tease, removing the red, lace bra and keeping my eyes on his as it fell to the floor.

His breath picked up.

I liked it.

My nipples perched, began to tingle... not at the cool air sweeping over my bare skin. At the fire of his gaze. I slowly pulled off my shoes, my pants, revealing nothing but a matching red thong. His hands curled to fists at his side, his jaw locked.

I stepped closer to him, slowly, demanding his eyes on my body.

"Off." His voice low, deep.

I slid out of my panties, tossed them to the side.

Breath escaped him.

Yes, come get me.

He took a step forward, I took a step back.

His brow arched.

I smirked.

He took another step, I backed up.

One more, then I slid onto the bed. "Your turn."

The corner of his lip curled, the cockiness that was Gage, then he slipped out of his shorts... and spandex.

It took everything in my power to keep my jaw from hitting the floor. I gaped at the length, the thickness of him, the pure manliness, unmatched.

Dear, God.

Locking onto his gaze, I laid back on the bed, my hands drifting to my breast, my finger circling around my nipple. He stared down at me, unmoving, watching, a king waiting for his show. Wanting more. Wanting to see what I could do.

Of course he did.

One hand working my breast, the other trailed down my belly, swirling around the tiny trail of hair. I lifted my legs, placing my feet on the edge of the bed, opening up to him. My skin flushed under his gaze, and I began to quiver with nothing more than the erotic show happening between us. How could I be so turned on without him even touching me?

A flush colored his neck.

I grinned.

My finger drifted lower, lower, until I felt the blissful zing of pleasure. Circling, I bit my lip. One finger dipped in.

He licked his lips.

Two fingers.

His hand drifted to his erection, a stroke to meet my own.

I groaned watching it.

And the groan did him in.

He closed the inches between us and gripped my thighs, spreading them wider, exposing all of me to him. I was wet, throbbing already, wanting, wanting, wanting.

Needing.

Desperate.

After sliding his hands under my ass, he gripped my waist and pulled me to the edge of the bed.

You're mine, the simmering look in his eyes told me.

Yes, I was.

His hands moved to my knees, widening even more, then pressing my legs back.

He got onto his knees.

My heart skipped a beat.

And then he devoured me.

His warm mouth closed over my sensitive skin, now tingling with friction. I gripped the bedspread the moment his tongue entered me, again, and again. I swayed under him, matching his rhythm. He wasn't done, God, he wasn't even close to being done. The warm, wet tip of his tongue trailed along my inner lips, hot, dripping wet, and finally, slid onto my clit. Warmth pooled between my legs as I began to throb with each racing beat of my heart.

He circled, softly, slowly at first. I squeezed my eyes shut, gripping the bedspread in a desperate attempt to release the sexual tension building at break-neck speed through my body. With his tongue lightly circling my clit, he inserted a finger, two... three. His pinky tickling farther below, tempting the forbidden spot.

I was on the brink of shattering.

"*Gage.*" His name rolled off my tongue in a desperate plea. "*Gage...*"

I screamed his name as the orgasm ripped through me.

My body fell limp with the euphoric release. Finally, I forced open my eyes. Gage stood over me, ripping off the top of a small, silver wrapper. He rolled on the condom like someone who knew what they were doing.

And my God, I wanted to know what this man could do.

He put his hands on my knees, pushed my legs open again, gripping, forcing them wider.

His tip found my opening, my breath hitched.

I opened wider to him, opening my legs, myself, my soul to him.

Take me.

Have me.

Make me yours.

He slid into me, his eyes drifting closed as I squeezed around him, tight, warm, wet with my orgasm.

"Fuck, Niki," he buried his face next to my ear and began the slow rhythm, the buildup to the storm.

"Open, Niki," he pleaded. "Open."

I arched my back and groaned as he reached depths I'd never felt before. I squeezed around him, wanting more even though I knew my body couldn't handle it. He settled into me, deep, hard, filling every inch of me.

"Niki," he breathed, dreamily.

He slid out, then back into me. Again, and again. And again.

His pace quickened, each thrust deeper than the last, each thrust opening me up more and more. Faster, harder, he pushed into me, removing my armor and stealing my breath.

Make me yours.

I tilted my chin up, offering my throat to him as my nails dragged down his back, slick with sweat, flexing with each movement. Stars burst in my eyes, fireworks, my body moving in waves with each thrust. His lips caressed my neck, the heat of his quick breaths matching my own. Dizzying, I wrapped my arms around him seeking any kind of control in a stormy ocean where we both were completely, utterly, lost in the moment. In one another. The bed shook, my head spun as he powered into me with the force only Gage Steele was capable of.

I closed my eyes, lost, drifting through the experience like a butterfly in the wind.

"Gage," I whined his name, panting.

"Again."

"Gage," I repeated, digging my fingernails into his skin, as the world began to spin around me.

"I'm yours. *Take me,* Gage. I'm yours."

Then, we shattered together.

Like fire and gasoline.

19

GAGE

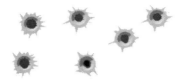

I stroked her hair, the soft brown silk weaving around my fingers, tickling my skin and making me want to rouse her for round two.

Three, I mean.

The moonlight bathed her naked body like liquid silver, emphasizing curves worthy of a goddess.

My goddess.

A sharp pang of possessiveness pulled me out of the moment like a baby being ripped from the womb.

She's. *Mine.*

I realized then, at that moment, I'd do anything to keep her. To protect her. Anything to keep her safe, happy.

Anything to keep her mine.

I'd give my life for hers. In a fucking heartbeat.

Worthy of that? Worthy of me? I inwardly laughed. Was *I* worthy of *her*?

The real question was, would she let me in?

Niki Avery had single-handedly stripped me of the armor I'd built around myself over the last year. Hell, maybe my whole life. As I gazed at her profile, so angelic, so serene,

I wondered why. What was different about this one? Why her?

Because it was *real*—emotional, for Christ's sake—the opposite of every conquest I'd had before... which were merely reasons to forget. To forget my mundane life. To forget my dad. To deaden the constant hurricane coursing through my veins. No, with Niki, I felt life. *Light.* Like my soul had been ripped from my chest, clutched in her hand, and kept for her keeping. Like I had given myself to her. And goddammit it felt good. It felt right.

It was the first time I actually *felt.*

I knew, at that moment, that I loved her. I knew it in every inch of my body.

I was in love with Niki Avery.

I couldn't help myself, and I leaned down and kissed her cheek.

She stirred, slowly turned her head and looked up at me with sleepy, satisfied eyes. Those lips curled upward, and mine did, too.

"How are you not asleep?"

I smiled, traced my finger down the slope of her nose.

"I can't sleep."

"You mean you don't sleep."

"Sometimes." My finger ran along the bruise below her eye, my gut clenching.

She gripped my hand. "Stop."

"I'll kill the guy who hurt you, Niki. I'll find him and I'll kill him."

"You'll find him, Gage, but you won't kill him." Her eyes narrowed with intensity, warning. Command. "I won't let you."

I stared back at her, her eyes locked onto mine daring me to challenge her. A moment slid between us, and it felt as though the last piece of metal slid down my body. I'd do whatever Niki Avery told me to do, or wouldn't, for that matter.

She smiled, releasing my hand and turning fully toward me, the moonlight illuminating her face.

I frowned, tilted my head, zeroing in on the bruise below her eye. My thoughts started to spin.

"You said he punched you, right?"

She nodded, a frown matching my own now.

"With his fist, right?"

"Is there any other way to punch someone?" She sat up. "What's going on?"

The wheels turned in my head.

"*Gage.* What?"

"He was directly in front of you, right? When he hit you?"

"Yes... where are you going with this?"

"Niki. Your attacker is left handed."

She gasped, covering her cheek with her hand. "Oh, my God you're right. The bruise would have been on the opposite side of my face."

"Exactly." I scrambled out of the bed. "We need to tell Lieutenant Colson and Haddix this immediately. This is a hell of a lead." I grabbed my shorts and searched the pockets. "Dammit, my phone is still outside the cage."

"The cage?"

"The wrestling ring in the back yard."

I'd left my freaking cell phone. Been completely out of reach for the last two hours. Not good when you ran a personal security company.

"Well, go get it. You need to tell them, now."

I hesitated, not wanting to leave.

"*Go.* Go get your phone. I'll be fine." She smirked, a sexy feline smirk. "You've got me completely exhausted. I might actually be able to sleep through the night." She crawled toward me, naked, then lifted up on her knees, tracing her finger down my stomach. A knot formed in my throat.

"Will you come back?"

My heart skipped a beat. A validation that she wanted me to come back. I leaned down and kissed her.

"Hell on earth couldn't keep me away. Give me twenty minutes."

"Good." She smiled. "In that case, bring food."

"I'll do that... and a bottle of champagne."

Her eyes sparkled with the smile on her face. My heart kicked. I reached down and plucked the security necklace off the floor and handed it to her. "Put this on. Always, keep it on."

"Yes, sir," she winked.

I grinned. "I like that. See you soon. Set the alarm behind me."

After confirming the alarm was set, I took the cart to the main house, stopping for my phone on the way in. Two new texts from Feen—

Text One: *Dad's office*

Text Two: *Come see me when you can - solo.*

I was instantly pulled back to reality, and instantly wanted to be back in Niki's bed. Twenty minutes. I could make a quick stop upstairs, then the kitchen, then get back to Cabin 1—with bells on.

I jogged up the steps feeling the most energy I'd felt

since I was back in Iraq, fighting for my country, my life. I was always on a high back then. But realizing I was in love with Niki was a freaking amazing high. A different high, but a high nonetheless. Fuck me if I didn't like that one better.

I pushed through the office door and found Phoenix in the exact place I'd left him earlier in the day.

Christ, had he been there all day?

"I found something..." his eyes sparked with excitement, and were no less heavy with exhaustion.

I crossed the room, concern quickening my steps.

Stacks of printouts covered Dad's desk, a cold cup of coffee sat on the edge. The same running code as earlier ran across the computer screens.

Feen pointed to one of the monitors. His hand was shaking.

"That secret code embedded in the satellites that I told you about..."

I went back in time, recalling the information that seemed so long ago. It felt like so much had happened since then. It had. I'd fallen in love.

"The code you think was used for communication regarding the assassination of Andrei Sokolov? The one you think has to do with the Knight Fox."

"Right. The dude who's going to wish he was never born if he really did kill Dad."

"Tell me you found him."

"Not yet, but, Gage... Dad had already started tracking him."

"Where? How?"

"Dad used a program he'd created and hacked into Sokolov's personal bodyguard's computer." He clicked on a new folder. "He copied encrypted emails, on and around the date of the assassination, that were signed *KF*..."

"Emails from the Knight Fox?"

"Right."

"So he tracked the Knight Fox's IP address?"

"No, that would have led him directly to Fox. Too easy, right? The Fox was using a web proxy to communicate, which hides the IP address. *But* Fox was using his cell phone to communicate and Dad was able to pin the tower the cell was pinging off of." He turned to me, his face paling. "Gage..."

A chill ran up my spine and for a moment, I didn't want to know. I didn't *want* to hear the words that were going to come out of my brother's mouth.

"The Knight Fox was *here.*"

"Here? *Where,* exactly, Feen?" My pulse picked up, along with a shot of anxiety.

"In freaking Berry Springs..."

I braced myself because I knew he wasn't done.

"Gage. The Fox was here... the day Dad died."

My heart stopped beating, my thoughts froze, my mouth unable to form a sentence, hell, even a single word.

A solid minute ticked by while my brother and I stared at each other.

"You believe me now, right? Dad was murdered for what he was investigating. And the Knight Fox is the one who did it."

My head bobbed up and down involuntarily. I realized then that I always had believed him.

Feen clapped his hands together in the first jolt of energy I'd seen in the last twenty-four hours. "I knew you would. Okay, so now we've got to somehow nail down this guy's IP address." He scrubbed his hands over his face and leaned forward, inches from the computer screen, and began typing.

"Feen."

He didn't look up. Didn't respond. He was already back in the zone.

"Feen," I said louder.

He looked up. Blinked.

"This a lot. We need to process. Plan. You need a break. Feen, you need a break."

"Breaks are for pussies."

"Then you're primed for one. You need sleep, Feen."

"Meh." He grabbed his coffee, noticed it was cold and scowled down at it.

"Let's get you some food and... ummm, I don't know... whatever that calming tea is... chamomile tea, or some shit."

"Who the fuck drinks chamomile tea?"

"People who need to relax... according to that commercial that runs on damn repeat."

"Pussies drink tea."

"You're *going* to drink tea. You're going to get the hell away from this room for a bit."

Feen sniffed, contemplated. "Whiskey."

"Fine. Deal. Let's go."

I hung back while Phoenix pulled himself out of Dad's chair, unsteady. Off.

I pretended to be looking at the scattered papers, then, as my brother moved away from the desk, I angled myself behind him in case the guy fell. In my thirty-three years of life, I'd never seen my brother so exhausted. So stressed. Weak, like he could fall over with a stiff gust of wind. Feen wasn't the type to show stress. Hell, none of us were. We'd work it out in the gym, or down at the shooting range, and that would be the end of it.

Not today.

We walked into the kitchen where Ax, still wearing a

leather jacket from an evening ride on the Harley, was pouring himself a drink. A tequila, reminding me we were *all* on edge. Not only because of Niki's attack, but something else. Something was in the air.

Something heavy.

"Jesus, dude, you okay?" Ax frowned, zeroing in on Feen.

"He's fine. Just needs something to eat, and a bed."

"Start with this." Ax forced his tequila into Feen's hand and flickered me a glance—*what the hell's going on?*

I wanted to tell him. I didn't. It wasn't the time. Hell, I needed a second to process.

Gunner sauntered in, chatting on his cell, and stopped in his tracks.

"Uh. I gotta go." He slid the phone into his pocket and stared at Feen, then looked back and forth between me and Ax.

I held up a hand and shook my head. *Not right now.*

We all got a drink, Ax and Gunner lingering at the countertop as I grabbed some leftover bacon and began making the Steele favorite—a BLT for my brother.

Feen dropped into a chair by a window and stared into the dark night. I felt Gunner's and Ax's curious—concerned —eyes on me. I glanced at them and nodded—*He's okay. Not now. Give him a sec.*

They nodded in return, then switched topics.

"How's Cabin 1?" Gunner asked.

"Niki," I replied, a bit too quickly. This earning simultaneous cocked brows from my brothers.

"Geez, Niki, *sorry.*"

I grabbed a knife, started chopping a tomato. Since when did I turn into a feminist? Most of my conquests were discussed by the color of their hair and shape of their breasts. *Love changes you,* my dad had once told me. I know

now that he was right. I popped some bread in the toaster and glanced at the clock. Twenty more minutes.

"Her attacker is left-handed." I said.

"How the hell do you know that?"

"From the location of the bruise on her face where the bastard clocked her. You guys heard from anyone tonight?"

"Spoke with Haddix a few hours ago." Ax grabbed a napkin and wrapped it around his sweating drink. "Mickey Greco lived two very different lives before he was busted for tax fraud. Dude was a model citizen, had a wife—who's since divorced his ass and moved to Hawaii—no children, but they were foster parents for multiple kids. Went to church, was part of the community, donated to local organizations, the whole deal."

Gunner sipped. "But behind closed doors, Greco was an evil bastard who tortured anyone who owed him money, and cut off his partner's head for uncovering his little side-business."

"Had someone *else* cut off her head," I corrected.

"Exactly. Haddix is still building a list of everyone associated with his business. The list is as long as my dick—"

"So not very."

"I said mine, not yours." Ax grinned, sipped. "Bottom line, according to every witness, Greco only had one trusted associate who knew the ins and outs of his drug business, and that guy got locked up with him."

"There's got to be a connection here. It's too big of a coincidence. Someone wants revenge for Greco being locked up." My brows knit together in concentration as I slapped together the rest of the sandwich and slid it in front of Feen, then yanked a beer from the fridge. "Family?"

"Just the wife in Hawaii. Colson confirmed her location."

I shook my head. "There's got to be something."

"Or, Niki's still lying, Gage." This comment barely audible from across the room.

I looked at the back of Feen's head. "She's not lying, Feen."

He didn't move, just kept his gaze out the window. "I don't know brother, I think this woman is good at manipulating people."

"What the hell's that supposed to mean?" I popped the top from my beer and tossed the cap across the room.

"Where have you been the last two hours?"

My stomach dropped. Gunner's and Ax's gazes shifted to me.

"What were you doing, Gage?" Feen's head turned, his eyes shaded by shadows.

I took a deep sip of beer... then lied. "Walking the grounds."

"Without your cell phone?"

Shit.

"Right after you made a complete ass of yourself in front of our visitor?"

Ax sucked in a breath beside me.

"Dude was her *ex-boyfriend,* Feen."

"Exactly. Someone who could have taken care of her. People who come to us have no one. The woman obviously doesn't care to be here. BSPD is handling the case. If you would have been thinking with your head, you would have sent her home with him."

I started to simmer. "She's being hunted, Feen."

"We protect people who want our protection, Gage." He shifted, his face sliding into the light. "Not people we want to fuck."

Anger spurt through my veins like a hit of cocaine. I slammed down my beer. "You think that's all this is?"

"I'm not going to repeat my question again, Gage. Where were you the last two hours?"

My eyes narrowed to slits, venom pooling in my mouth. "Not trying to convince my little brother that Dad was killed, that's for damn sure." The words spit from my mouth.

Feen's fist slammed onto the table, sending it on its side. He sprang to his feet and turned toward me. "Fuck *you*, Gage. I told you not to say anything. And where were you? You were fucking Niki Avery in her cabin." His hands curled into fists as he slowly crossed the kitchen, like a panther on the hunt.

I set down my bottle, feeling my brothers shift closer to me.

Feen continued, a distant, crazed look in his eyes. "The only thing that would pull you away from your cell phone is a tight hole and willing mouth. You had sex with a client, in her cabin. In the place where the client is supposed to be protected. You crossed your final fucking line."

"You're out of your fucking mind. Brother." I shifted to the balls of my feet.

"I might be out of my mind but at least I've still got my dignity. I said yesterday that you were just like Dad. I was wrong. Dad would be ashamed of you."

I lunged forward sending my drink shattering onto the floor. Everything flashed around me—Ax barreling into me, wrapping his arms around me from behind. Gunner took Feen, wrestling him to the ground.

I twisted under my twin brother's hold.

"Stop," Ax demanded calmly in my ear. "Relax. Take a breath, brother, cool it. He's not right."

I stopped fighting and focused on his words, the low timbre of his voice.

"Cool it, Gage. He's not right." Ax repeated.

I forced my eyes closed and inhaled deeply through my nose. A deep breath, then another.

Ax released me.

On the floor next to us, Gunner was muttering something to Feen and I assumed it was along the same lines as Ax had said to me. Then, he lifted off him. Phoenix scrambled up and turned to me, his chest heaving.

We stared at each other as Gunner and Ax began picking up the shards of glass on the floor.

What. The fuck. Just happened.

I tore my eyes away and shook my head. *"Screw this,"* I muttered, then walked out of the kitchen, leaving the crazy-ass chaos behind. Emotions swirled as I pushed through the front door and stepped into the cool, dark night.

Dad would be disappointed.

It was true, but my relationship with Niki wasn't the only reason the man would have been let down. It had been many, many years since I'd seen that look in my older brother's eyes. What if Gunner and Ax hadn't been there? Dad was probably rolling over in his grave. He'd have our hides if he knew his sons were fighting. *Really* fighting, not bullshit sibling arguments.

God, I missed him.

I looked up at the stars twinkling around a full moon.

Dad. *Murdered?*

The thought made me sick to my stomach.

I closed my eyes and took a deep breath... then another...

My eyes popped open and darted around the landscape. I inhaled again, smelling fumes from a vehicle.

I yanked my phone and called Wolf.

"Hey, what're—"

"Go check the security system."

"Why?" I heard shuffling through the phone.

"Someone just drove by. Either up the driveway or on the road below."

A second passed as Wolf logged into the system. "You're right. A black and white passed by and..." a few more clicks. "Took a left toward the cabins. About five minutes ago."

"A cop car?"

"Yeah. Silhouette looks like Haddix behind the wheel."

My brow furrowed as I stared down the driveway. What the hell was Haddix doing visiting the compound at nine at night?

More importantly, where was he going?

20

NIKI

I ran my fingers over my lips and a small smile crossed my face. I could still taste him, still feel his lips on mine. My body was a mixture of bubbling excitement and languid relaxation. I glanced at the clock for the hundredth time since Gage had left the cabin.

Ten more minutes.

Another smile, and it took everything I had not to reach below the covers and explore myself. Never, in my entire life, had I been turned on like that. Never had I felt that kind of connection, a kind of kindred spirit so intense it melted my thoughts, worries, concerns, and left me with nothing but my soul lying right there on the bed, ready, willing, hell, *screaming* for him to take it.

Gage Steele had picked me up, flipped me over, and turned me on my head.

It felt one-hundred percent *right*.

I sat up in bed, too giddy to sleep. Maybe a quick jump in the shower to refresh... maybe a quick drink before he came back. Stumbling out of bed, I grabbed my Steele Security T-shirt. It felt like silk falling over my skin, my bare breasts. It was like I was on some psychedelic drug, my body lustfully responding to any kind of stimulus. I placed my hand on my stomach and smiled, noting the soreness below.

I touched my lips, thinking of his on mine.

I wanted him again.

And again, and again.

Ten minutes.

Resigning to the cold hard fact that I was alone, I slipped on a pair of shorts, then padded to the kitchen.

A pair of headlights twinkling through the trees grabbed my attention. I frowned and glanced at the back door, where Gage usually parked his ATV.

Not Gage.

My hand drifted to my security necklace, fingering the red button as I walked to the front door and peered out the window, knowing that whoever was coming up the drive could see my silhouette against the lighted background.

The black and white colors registered as the car rolled to a stop. The police. I exhaled a breath of relief, and watched Officer Haddix, dressed in plain clothes, unfold himself from the driver's side, carrying a large bag and gruff look on his face. He stepped into the light pooling from the porch, pale skin marked by deep circles under his eyes. I could only hope it was because he'd spent the last twenty-four hours working like a dog on my case.

Our eyes met through the window and I unlocked the door.

"Evening, officer."

"Miss Avery," he nodded and stopped at the threshold. "Sorry to stop by so late."

"No problem at all." I stepped back and offered him inside. "Is there something new with the case?"

"Not that I can discuss." He stepped inside.

"So, that's a no."

Avoiding the question, he glanced at the empty beer bottles next to my laptop. "I see you're settling in."

"It's a nice place. To escape, anyway."

His gaze lifted to the cracked windows from the gunshots the night before. "Bullet proof windows help."

"It's like Fort Knox in here."

Amusement flickered on his face. "I'm sure it is. The Steele brothers don't cut corners... with their business anyway." He shifted his gaze to me, scanning me from head to toe before saying, "Just be careful with Gage, okay?"

"What do you mean, exactly?"

"You've been through a lot, Miss Avery. The Steele brothers have a reputation in this town. Gage... *had drinks* with my cousin a few months back. Never spoke to her again. Honestly, I don't like the guy." His jaw twitched. "The last thing you need is to have your heart broken."

A strange defensiveness, a protectiveness over the misunderstood man I'd just slept with, crept through my system. I knew about Gage's escapades. I also knew what had just happened between us. I knew I loved him.

"I can handle picking up the pieces."

"Don't say I didn't warn you."

"Officer Haddix, did you come here to tell me not to sleep with Gage Steele, or perhaps you had something else related to my attack that *is* your business."

His brow cocked, a slight smile crossing his face. He chuckled. "With that little attitude, maybe Gage has met his match. Anyway, yes and no, I did come by to warn you about Gage, but also..." he handed me the bag he'd been holding. "Here's the keys to your car, your purse, and cell phone. Your car's outside the station, ready for you whenever."

I grabbed the bag like contraband. "Oh my God, thank

you. Did you find anything? Prints on the car, my things, anything?"

His lips thinned as he shook his head.

"Damn. Well, thank you."

"You're welcome. I was in the area, anyway. On my way to check on my nephew who's camping on the river. Rowdy boys they are. Then, back to town. Would you like me to take you to your car? It'd be no problem at all."

I glanced out the window toward the main house, my stomach twisting at the thought of leaving Gage. Not tonight. Not yet.

"No, actually, I can get it tomorrow."

"Okay, then. Have a good one." He turned.

"Officer Haddix?"

He paused.

"Thank you. Not only for bringing by my things... for the fair warning."

He looked over his shoulder and winked. "You're a tough one, Avery. Just keep your eyes open."

"Will do."

GAGE

"Hey." Ax pushed out the front door and walked down the steps. "You okay?"

"Yeah." Truth was, I'd already forgotten about the bullshit argument in the kitchen. "Hey, you said you talked to Haddix today, right?"

"Yeah, why?"

I glanced back toward the dirt road at the bottom of the hill. "Any idea why he'd want to talk to Niki right now?"

"Not sure; mentioned to me that he was going to check on her Jeep at some point today." He shrugged. "Could be a million reasons to talk to her right now."

He had a point.

"Go check on her... you whipped son of a bitch." Grinning, Ax picked up the foam football and chucked it at me.

I froze as the ball fell to my feet.

My blood turned ice cold.

"What?" Ax frowned.

My thoughts were a jumbled circus, racing faster than I could push out the words. "Niki's attacker was left handed..."

"Yeah, you mentioned that..."

The vision of the football spiraling into the woods earlier flashed through my head like a horror movie on loop. My brother's voice faded behind me as I spun on my heel and sprinted to Ax's Harley that was still parked outside.

Paul Taylor was left-handed.

NIKI

I watched Haddix's car disappear down the driveway, and after shutting and locking the door, the low grumble of a truck pulled my attention back outside.

Another vehicle came inching up the driveway, this one a truck. My mouth dropped.

I pushed through the door. "What the *hell* are you doing here?"

Paul Taylor, the ex-boyfriend who apparently couldn't let go, slid out of his truck and shut the door.

"I came by to talk." His eyes locked on me as he crossed the gravel.

"Talk to me again? Listen, Paul, we ended weeks ago. I don't know why you can't let go. I've got a lot I'm dealing with—"

"I'm sure you do. Locking away good people, destroying lives."

"What are you talking about?" I scanned the woods for Gage.

"Mickey Greco was a good man, Niki." Paul stepped onto the porch. "Like a father to me." His face flushed a deep red, matching the fire in his eyes. "He and his wife took me in when my parents died. They were my foster family for three years when I was in elementary school. They took me in when no one else did."

My heart started to pound as I reached for my necklace with one hand and slowly inched backward searching for the door knob with the other.

He continued, "You never noticed that I asked you out right when you started poking around in Mickey's life, huh?"

My finger slammed the red *SOS* button on the pendant. Keep him talking, was all I could think. Keep him talking until Gage got there.

"You started dating me to get close to Mickey's case. See my cards." My hand slid over the knob, my back against the door.

"Trust me, I'da liked to see more than just your cards. Unfortunately, your pussy's locked up as tight as your laptop was." He inched closer. "There were three things Mickey taught me. One, always have someone do your dirty work. Well, you went and killed that bastard last night. Two... loyalty or death."

My heart slammed against my ribcage.

"And three, Mickey taught me the importance of teaching people their lessons." He stepped closer. "Here's yours."

The light reflected off the barrel of a pistol as Paul pulled it from his belt. Panic ripped through me and I lunged to the side as the blast pierced my eardrums, the bullet shattering the wood on the front door.

I scrambled backward, until my spine hit the deck railing.

Paul spun toward me, gun raised, eyes wild. I was backed

into the corner, literally, with no way to protect myself and nowhere to run.

Fight, or die.

Fight, or die, I told myself.

Flashbacks of the knife piercing Ian's neck, the feeling when the blade cut through the skin, the blood squirting out, the images spun in my head, inciting a blow of adrenaline through my veins.

The human need for survival.

I leapt forward, grabbing for the gun. Our bodies collided with the force of two sumo wrestlers in the ring. The gun flew from his hand, skipping across the wood slats. We both turned and dove for it, swatting, grasping, reaching until it tumbled off the deck and disappeared in the darkness. He grabbed my legs, pulling me backward, shards of wood slicing my skin like tiny blades. I twisted on my side and dragged my fingernails down his neck.

He threw himself off me. "You fucking bitch."

As I scrambled up, I caught the glimpse of a flower pot a split second before it slammed into my skull.

21

GAGE

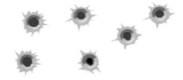

*T*he wind whipped around me like ice over my heated skin as I sped through the woods with only the headlight from Ax's Harley cutting through the dark night. Ax was somewhere behind me, the others were on their way.

Over the rumble of the motorcycle, a gunshot echoed through the air like a missile through my gut. My heart stopped, followed by a kickstart of panic, racing like a meth overdose. The bike ramped a rock, and I struggled to stay upright. Not ideal conditions for a motorcycle. Correction, worst conditions ever for a bike. I frantically scanned the woods, looking for Paul, for Niki.

Shadows from the full moon slinked from tree to tree, teasing me, taunting me.

Fucking Paul Taylor.

I ground my teeth so hard I was sure I cracked a tooth.

Paul Taylor.

Hold on Niki, I repeated over and over. *Hold on. I'm coming.* The moonlight caught a flash of metal ahead of me —a truck hauling ass down the mountain on a trail we only ever used for our ATV's. I cranked the bars, weaving through the trees, following the taillights. Faster, faster, knowing I had the advantage because I knew every tree, boulder, and dip on this mountain.

As I came up behind him, the light reflected off a four-wheeler secured in the bed—a Polaris Sportsman. The same one captured on our security cameras. The same one that carried the bastard that shot at Niki.

Niki.

He had her, I knew it in my gut. I darted around the trees and pulled up beside the truck, inches from the door. I looked inside, and my stomach dropped to my feet.

Niki's body lay crumpled in the passenger seat, her head dangling above the floor mat as if her neck had been snapped. Her eyes were closed, mouth open. My chest constricted with panic. I stood, leaning my body forward and pressed the throttle, knowing I was going way too fast for the terrain.

Paul looked at me from behind the wheel. My veins burst with rage.

Yeah fucker, I got you.

I ramped a fallen log, and noted the location—we were only a few yards away from a deep ravine, almost impossible to see in the night. Based on how fast Paul was driving, he had no idea what laid before him. At the speed we both were going, there was no way in hell to survive that tumble.

My heart hammered trying to put together thoughts, a plan, to prevent Niki from going off the cliff.

Trees zoomed past.

Ten seconds.

I looked at Niki.

So beautiful, so perfect. Taken. Taken from me.

Fury dissolved my thoughts, my rationale, my common

sense as the bike seemed to guide itself, pulling ahead of the truck. I gritted my teeth and focused on the massive boulder ahead.

The world stopped around me, my vision tunneled, my mind focused only on doing whatever I had to do to keep Niki from going over that ledge.

Hail Mary.

I pulled up on the handlebars and ramped the boulder, hurling my body off the bike mid-air and landing in the yellow pool of headlights as the truck barreled toward me.

Hail Mary.

With an ear-piercing whine, the Harley flew off the cliff behind me. Paul swerved and slammed into a tree.

The driver's door flew open and Paul jumped out in an attempt to flee, but not before I grabbed the fucker by the hair and slammed his face into the tree. His eyes rolled into the back of his head moments before his body crumpled to the ground.

"Niki!" I jumped into the truck and crawled to her limp body. Blood streaked her face, her clothes. Flashes of war, death, destruction played like a movie on fast forward through my head.

"Niki, please, *God,* Niki..." I wrapped her in my arms, tears stinging my face.

"Niki..."

The moonlight danced across her face, pale, gaunt, lifeless.

"Niki... *shit,* Niki."

I pulled her to my chest, and her eyes slowly opened.

22

NIKI

1 week later...

The last of the waning sun sparkled along the forest floor, golden spotlights swaying in the cool breeze.

I zipped up my jacket.

"You cold?" Gage broke his stride and looked over.

I smiled at how in tune he'd become with me over the last week. So very un-Gage-like.

"No, I'm fine, but would be much better if you'd tell me where we were going." I looked around at the miles and miles of woods around us, painted with the colors of fall.

He smiled. "Almost there."

Pine needles crunched under my hiking boots—the shoes Gage had demanded I wore for his little impromptu, surprise trip. He'd shown up, all leather and motorcycle, at my house an hour earlier, told me to get dressed for a hike and didn't take no for an answer.

Very Gage-like.

He'd driven me to the compound, past the cabins, switched to an ATV, then parked that, and got out on foot with nothing but a basket in his hand and sparkle in his eye.

We'd been walking for about ten minutes, when I zeroed in on a boulder, marked by blurred landscape beyond that. A weird deja vu gripped me. I frowned, looking at him.

"The ravine?"

He nodded.

"The ravine where you saved my life?"

A slight nod, with a twitch of his jaw.

My frown deepened as we drew nearer to the eighty-foot drop-off that almost took my life, and Gage's as well.

My stomach clenched as the memories of the last week started barreling through my head.

Paul Taylor, an orphan of two drug-addicted parents, was taken in by Mickey Greco and his picture-perfect wife when he was a young, impressionable boy. Lived with them for three years until he was shuffled elsewhere, but not before forming a life-long bond with the psychotic bastard. Over the course of the last week, we'd learned that Mickey had kept in close contact with Paul, slowly—and secretly— grooming him to take over his drug business. They'd become thick as thieves, with Paul using his law education as leverage in the business.

Enter me, Niki Avery.

Paul had attached himself to me the moment he'd found out I was working the case against Mickey. The drinks, dinners, dancing were all a ruse for Paul to get as close to the case as possible, doing whatever he could to save his prodigal father from being locked up.

When I won the case and Mickey got locked away, Paul began plotting his revenge.

Enter Gage Steele—and the end to Paul's freedom.

Paul had been thrown behind bars and was likely to remain there for life, just like his mentor, who was about to face a slew of evidence pulled from Paul's computer proving that Mickey had ordered Paul to kill his business partner, Sheila Cancio, when she'd uncovered his side-business.

Poetic justice.

And there I was, a week later, the bruises beginning to fade, the cuts beginning to heal, picking up the pieces of my new life one by one, with Gage never leaving my side.

I was due back full-time at work in a few days, but not before a walk in the woods with Gage, apparently.

I'd take it.

"Hungry?" He asked.

I grinned. "I could eat."

He grinned back and winked. "Good." He stopped at the edge of the ravine. "We're here."

As I looked over the edge, imagining the fall, Gage laid a red flannel blanket on a smooth rock, followed by the basket. He shrugged out of his leather jacket, and wrapped it around my shoulders from behind, the close proximity of him sending a shiver down my spine.

His lips tickled my ear lobe, and my body responded, warming below in record time. Gage Steele had an unearthly power over my body. That was just fine with me.

"Sit, please," he whispered softly.

I turned my head with a smile. "Good job."

"Thanks. Working on my inner feminist."

I rolled my eyes and sank to the blanket. "It's not a feminist to be polite."

"Hey, I've always been polite to you."

"Demanding."

"Fine. I'm working on my demanding...ness."

"As you should," I winked.

He opened the flaps of the woven basket—the kind that reminded me of a fifties-era black and white romance. The juxtaposition of the burly, badass alpha male and the delicate picnic basket had my heart kicking.

"You made me a picnic..." I smiled and leaned closer to him, wanting to toss the basket aside and pull him on top of me.

"Don't get too excited, sweetheart..."

I let the *sweetheart* slide.

"It's BLT's, chips, and, most importantly..." He pulled out a bottle of expensive champagne.

I laughed. "BLT's, huh?"

"I don't cook."

"I do."

"Thank God." He smirked.

I assumed he'd had Dallas or Celeste put together the basket, but after handing me a sandwich wrapped in paper towels and an unzipped baggie of crushed chips, I knew that was all Gage. And that, *that,* made me fall in love with him even more.

With a *pop,* the cork flew into the air and disappeared over the ravine. As he poured the three-hundred dollar champagne, I asked, "Why here?"

He said nothing for a moment, his brows knitting together in concentration.

Finally... "I grew up here. In these woods." He handed me a cup of bubbly, settled back and sipped. I wasn't used to this Gage, a calmer, more reflective man than the one I'd met in the woods a week earlier.

I liked it.

"My dad used to take us hiking every week," he continued. "Every single week. Said it was important to know our land and what we owned like the back of our hands. And we do, all of us, we know every inch of this land." He chuckled. "When we were little, Phoenix would drop us miles from the house, blindfold us, then turn us loose. Last one home had to do the chores for a week. And if we took off the blindfold? A full month of chores."

"Let me guess, you won?"

He laughed again, staring into the woods. "No, actually, that always went to Ax. That guy is one with nature." He flashed me a devilish grin. "I was always the one who peeked."

I laughed. "Doing whatever you needed to do to get the job done."

He nodded, sipped.

"So, back to the original question. Why here?"

The paper cup twisted in his hands. "Because I refuse to let the last memory of this place be a bad one. This place..." he looked around at the dirt and fallen leaves. "This very spot has changed my life, forever." His voice cracked. It took all my strength to hide my surprise at the emotion he was displaying. I placed my hand over his.

He looked at me, the intensity behind his stormy eyes making my stomach sink. "You've changed my life, Niki."

Tears welled up. "You saved mine."

He set down his drink and pulled out a small, light blue box from the basket. "And I always will."

My heart officially stopped beating.

He handed the little blue box to me, steady hands, confident. Melting.

My hands, on the contrary, were trembling as I pulled the blue ribbon and opened the box.

Inside laid a delicate diamond necklace with a red ruby pendant... exactly like the security necklace I'd worn when I was in Cabin 1... except exponentially more expensive. My breath caught in a gasp.

I pulled it from the box. "Gage... this is..."

"For you. I will always protect you, Niki." He took it from my hands and turned over the pendent, revealing a small, black button. "It has the same call button as the other." His eyes sparked. "I will *always* be there for you."

Breathless, I threw my arms around him, inhaling the fresh musk that was Gage. Always Gage.

"There's something else." He pulled a larger box from the basket, this one wrapped in old, faded newspaper.

I beamed from ear-to-ear. "Another gift?"

He handed it to me. "Not the best wrapper, sorry. Open it."

Smiling like a kid on Christmas morning, I unwrapped the gift... revealing a box of dirt.

I cocked a brow and tilted my head. "Uh... thanks?"

He smiled. "The gift is what's in it."

"Ants?"

He laughed, leaned closer. "The seed to a red maple tree."

My heart dropped to my feet, along with my jaw.

"Now you can have all the red leaves you want."

"Gage," breathless, I stared at him.

He took the box, cupped my face in his hands, his eyes swimming.

"Niki Avery, I love you. I didn't save your life. You saved mine."

Tears fell down my face. Yes, my life had changed. And I now, I couldn't wait for the future.

"I love you, too, Gage."

GAGE

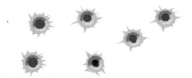

*I*t was almost ten in the evening by the time Niki and I had made it back to the house. Diamonds, dirt, and champagne set the scene for a decent dinner and explosive sex under the sunset. Then, some more, under the stars. I was happy, languid, content. Three things I hadn't felt in a very long time.

Ax, Gunner, and Dallas had taken to the kitchen for a nightcap.

Me? I'd taken Niki into my arms and carried her upstairs to my bedroom.

"No cabin?" She said softly against my chest, the buzz of champagne and orgasms making her beautiful eyes swim.

"No cabin. You're under my lock and key now." I flipped back the covers of my four-poster king bed and laid her down. She looked up at me with tired, happy eyes.

A knot grabbed my throat and for the second time that evening, hell, maybe for the second time in my life, I felt the sting of tears. I leaned down, kissing her forehead softly, and whispered, "I love you, Niki. I fucking love you, so much."

"I love you, too, Gage."

It wasn't five minutes later that she fell asleep. I stroked her hair watching the heavy rise and fall of her chest until I was certain she was in a deep sleep, a happy, restorative sleep. I kissed her one more time, inhaling the scent of her shampoo, the scent of my Niki.

"I'll be back," I whispered.

One last look and I quietly padded out of the room, clicking the door closed behind me.

The hallway was dark, the house silent, still. Not a sound anywhere, not the low hum of a television, music, conversation in the kitchen. Nothing.

An eerie stillness grabbed me, an instinct, a gut feeling that something wasn't right.

I paused, standing motionless, listening to the deafening silence around me, feeling the heaviness of the air.

My pulse picked up, and that alarmed me. No, something wasn't right.

I looked up and down the hall, my gaze landing on Dad's office at the end, and the dim glow underneath the door.

Like a magnet, I made my way past the staircase, each step quicker than the last. Tunnel visioned, everything around me started to blur. I broke out in a jog.

As I neared the last door on the left, the thrum of my pulse echoed in my head like a war drum, moments before a bloodbath.

"Feen?" I turned the knob, the hammer in my chest almost crippling.

The door creaked open.

My eyes locked on my brother, slumped over our father's chair, with a bullet in his head.

******

Ready for Ax's story?

From bestselling and multi-award-winning romantic suspense author Amanda McKinney comes the second book in the steamy, edge-of-your-seat, three-part series, Steele Shadows Security...

Hidden deep in the remote mountains of Berry Springs is a private security firm where some go to escape, and others find exactly what they've been looking for.

Welcome to Cabin 1, Cabin 2, Cabin 3...

Always be prepared, that was Axel Steele's motto. While his brothers were throwing down at the local bar, Ax was the guy in the background devising the getaway plan. Dubbed "the smart one," the former special-ops Marine believed in structure and routine, a way of life the universe seemed hellbent on challenging. Amidst a firestorm of family drama, Ax finds a woman held captive in the middle of the woods, and in desperate need of his help. With an armful of tattoos as colorful as her attitude, his new client is his antithesis—a free-spirited, spontaneous hippie that tests every bit of his patience... and his self-restraint.

Erika Zajac has been living life on her own terms since she was just sixteen. But her gypsy lifestyle came to a screeching halt when the horrific past she'd tried so hard to bury came back in the form of chains and cuffs. Suddenly, Erika finds herself under the security—and scrutiny—of a temperamental bodyguard with the emotional capacity of a rock, and six-pack to match. But no amount of brains or brawn was going to distract her from her goal, or the secrets she'd kill to keep.

Deceit, lies, wrath. Ax's client had them all. The only question was, which of Erika's deadly sins would she choose? Revenge... or him?

Grab your copy of Cabin 2 today!

SNEAK PEEK

Cabin 2 (Steele Shadows Security)
Chapter 1

Erika

My lungs burned as I sprinted up the mountain, my pulse drowning out the thrum of bugs around me. A bead of sweat rolled down my face, followed by another. I didn't wipe it, I didn't care. Cross-training was not the place for babies. In fact, I kind of liked it because sweat was proof that I was pushing myself to the limits, and that's exactly what I intended to do. I'd been told it was the steepest mountain in the area. What I hadn't been told was that thing was almost vertical, and the "jogging trails" were nothing more than a rocky path cut out of dense forest. That was fine though. My quads were on fire, but that was fine, too. No gain without pain. An overused cliché, but it was true. I had to believe that something good came from pain. That *all* pain somehow had its purpose. Yin and yang. If only that saying were true for everything in life. If only *all* pain really did lead to gain.

Because I was a walking example that it didn't.

Another bead down my forehead, this one dripping off my nose. I let it go without swiping it, then let another one drip. Just let it go, I thought. As if the universe awarded me for my sweat-accepting badassery, a gust of wind swept past me, cooling my slicked skin. I breathed in the crisp air, the spicy scent of fall. I'd ditched my jacket somewhere along the trail mid-mountain. It pained me to toss the brand-new windbreaker, but I could always get another, more often than not, at no cost. A bonus to my fitness obsession was that I'd gotten to know the manager at the local athletic store personally, and in my bed. Free samples and stamina. Heck of a combination. Besides, if someone took the jacket it must be because they needed it. It was my gift to them. A good deed is never lost. Right, universe?

I ground my teeth and focused on the crest of the mountain where the trail evened out, then disappeared into the trees again.

Pat, pat, pat, my running shoes pounded the pine needles beneath me. My legs tingled with fatigue, a familiar feeling giving me that extra push to finish.

Screw you mountain, I repeated over and over, my heart feeling like it was about to explode in my chest. Another blast of wind, except this time it felt like I was running through a wall of water. I see you, universe, and I raise you. A blow of adrenaline had me pushing harder as the wind continued to challenge me, this time with a tornado of crisp orange and red leaves swirling around me. One pelted me directly in the forehead, hellbent on breaking my focus.

Bastard.

Beautiful bastard, but one nonetheless.

Come on, come on, endorphins burst through my veins, carrying me up the last few yards until finally, I crested the top of the mountain.

I doubled over, chest heaving, and checked my watch.

Record broken.

I sputtered a maniacal sounding laugh and straightened. A trio of birds darted away in response.

I'd beaten my personal best and it felt good.

Damn. Good.

I'd been told The Red Rock trail was infamous for its steep climbs and brutal switchbacks—and today proved that to be true. A total of fifteen miles roundtrip through one of the most treacherous mountains in Berry Springs. Cliffs, valleys, caves, boulders, a new obstacle every turn, it seemed. And that was good, exactly what I needed, because the annual Hippie Harvest race was coming up in a few weeks and finishing second place again was as acceptable as a tattoo inked by a drunken artist. Trust me on that.

I put my hands on my hips and did a slow turn. The wind whistled through the trees above me, birds chattering, squirrels scurrying. The sound of nature, a stillness, a calmness that only Mother Nature could provide. My gaze landed on a glorious sugar maple tree, a shimmering gold under the late afternoon sun. I traced the glowing silhouette in my mind, like a brush on a canvas, taking note of the various shades, textures, each coming together in a brilliant display.

A crow called out, its haunting caw pulling my attention behind me.

I frowned, the high from my jog beginning to waver.

Where the heck was I?

Thirty minutes earlier, I'd decided it was a great idea to veer off the trail and blaze my own path up the mountain in an attempt to challenge myself. Nothing like un-manicured trails to kick the burn up a notch. The problem was, I hadn't marked my route.

I glanced up at the waning sun, hanging above a mountain peak in the distance. Dusk was approaching and I guessed I had about an hour of daylight left. Better get a move on. Although I wasn't sure where I was, I knew that *down* was the best way to find myself. After a few gulps of water, I started back down the mountain. Minutes passed as I focused on my steps against the dirt, suddenly aware of how alone I was. No voices, laughter, joggers, or hikers. No rumbles of engines, dirt bikes, giggling children, nothing.

The breeze had stilled, halted, along with every creature around me it seemed. No squirrels, birds.

Nothing.

I glanced over my shoulder, my stomach tickling with nerves. How had I ventured so far from the trail? As much as I'd like to say that it wasn't like me to be that irresponsible, making decisions without thinking them through was kind of my thing. I'd followed a whim; gone in the direction that I was pulled, as I always did. And that blessed spontaneity had gotten me lost... again. Spontaneity, or, reckless impulsion as my brother would call it.

My psychologist called it restlessness.

But a life filled with schedules, meetings, endless events, mindless small talk, shameless butt-kissing? That kind of lifestyle went to my brother. Spending days behind a computer, analyzing reports, drowning in unread emails? No. No, that wasn't me. I'd rather play the starring role in an eighties sex-ed film for high school students than spend my days behind glowing monitors.

Me? Eccentric, beatnik, flighty, flower child, and my personal favorite—Beverly Hills Boho. Those were a few of the names I'd been called, although I preferred free-spirit. I took life as it came, one day at a time, a notion that was nothing less than alien to my elitist upbringing.

One day at a time. I knew all too well that life was too short not to stop and smell the roses. A mantra I'd set in stone the day I turned sixteen, stole my father's credit card and caught the first flight to Europe with nothing but a carry on. A Louis Vuitton carry-on, but carry-on nonetheless. I'd made it through Greece, Bulgaria, and was on my way to Istanbul when I encountered a young, handsome, yet prickly-looking fellow sent by my father to pack me up and send me home. His latest and greatest Harvard educated intern, I'd learned. So, after a few nights showing him more than just the sights, I'd packed up and journeyed home, leaving Jake-the-intern heartbroken in the penthouse suit of the Royal Palace, and my mini-crisis in the rearview mirror. I'd arrived home to frozen credit cards and a note that told me to get a real job.

So, I'd traded the Cartier watch dear Daddy had gotten me for my thirteenth birthday for a rusted Volkswagen hatchback* and crossed the border, earning me fluency in Spanish and a wicked case of food poisoning.

And I never took a single penny from him again. Not one single penny from the Zajac fortune.

Water off a duck's back, that was my motto.

That was my motto the day I'd challenged myself on Red Rock Trail.

That was my motto the day that unearthed a past I'd tried so desperately to forget.

Bracing myself on a sapling, I edgèd over a boulder, sliding on loose rocks. The terrain was becoming rockier, steeper, and I had no memory of the area. A tingle of fear, maybe more like awareness, slid up my spine. And looking back, that was the moment—the moment that I should have beelined it down the mountain without looking back. Trusted my instinct—that little warning bell.

Did I? Of course not.

I picked my way through the brush, shadows from the slanting sun swaying back and forth in a breeze I didn't feel. The world was darkening around me, as if I needed anything else to add to the sudden creep-factor I was feeling.

Clank, clank, clank...

I froze, my ears perking at the pitched sound breaking the eerie silence of the woods.

Clank, clank, clank...

A tapping, in perfect repetition, somewhere in the distance.

Metal on metal.

What the heck was metal on metal in the middle of nowhere?

My wildest dreams, my most terrifying nightmares couldn't prepare me for what happened next.

Perhaps it was my naturally inquisitive side that, according to my dad I'd gotten from my mom, but, true to Erika Zajac form—and against all better judgement—I veered off course, again, and followed the noise.

Clank, clank, clank...

I came up on a small clearing, confident the banging was becoming louder, and more confident that it was coming from underground.

My pulse started to pick up as I stepped out of the cover of the tree line, exposing myself to whatever was triggering my sudden anxiety. I stood out in the open feeling like I was stark-raving naked at the Super Bowl. I looked around the circle of woods lining the clearing, darkening in the shadows.

Again, good time to turn around and go back.

Nope. Not me. Not this genius.

I forced one foot in front of the other, picking my way to the middle of the clearing.

Clank, clank, clank...

The incessant tapping now becoming one with my thudding heartbeat, I stepped up to a boulder, extended to tiptoes and peeked over, half expecting the headless horseman to jump out. Instead, what I got was the corner of a small trap door covered in dead leaves and twigs.

My eyes popped. A trap door in the middle of the woods?

Clank, clank...

The noise was coming from whatever was behind that door. Whatever the heck was locked deep underground.

I looked around again, pulling my cell phone from the pocket of my leggings.

No reception. Of course.

I focused back on the door, chewing a hole in the bottom of my lip.

Clank, clank...

Pushing the apprehension aside, because God knew I was good at that, I shoved my cell back into my pocket and scrambled over the rock. A thin beam of sunlight, I swear the last beam of the day, shone like a beacon onto the door. Like a magnet pulling me to it.

Okay, universe, I remember thinking as I swept away the debris revealing a metal lock—*new*. A brand-new metal lock on a rusty trap door deep in the mountains.

The clanking had stopped at this point, and I found

myself desperate to hear it again for some odd reason. Desperate to ensure what it was, was okay.

Like it was my very own mission.

It was a key lock, not a combination. I'd picked a number of locks in my day, most notably when I'd forgotten my keys on my way for a night out. How could this be different? I huffed out a breath, and as if accepting the challenge —and now wanting to know more than ever what was in there—I went in search for something to pick it.

Nine twigs, one narrow rock, and dusk officially settling into the woods later, the lock gave with a loud *pop*, second only to the skipping of my heart.

My hands were unsteady as I removed the shiny metal and set it aside.

It was then, I had a moment. *Stay or leave. Stay or leave, Erika.*

With a defiant inhale—because only crazy people listened to the voices in their heads—I grabbed the flat, thin handle and lift*ed* the door. The musty scent of damp earth wafted into my face as I peered at the narrow, wooden ladder fading into a pitch-black hole in the ground.

The first thing I noticed was that the ladder also appeared to be new, and clean. That, along with the lock, confirmed my suspicions that despite the remote location of the place, someone was actively using it.

Or, hiding something in it.

I glanced over one shoulder, then the other, my mind racing.

I turned back to the hole, the clanking sound looping on repeat in my head as I contemplated what to do.

Taking a deep breath, I leaned in. *"Hello?"* I cringed at my voice echoing off the once quiet woods like a foghorn announcing my location. Announcing that I was snooping somewhere that, I knew, one-hundred percent, I shouldn't be.

No response from the pit.

I gripped the sides and stuck my head inside, and called out again. Still nothing.

With a clench of my jaw, I shuffled, lowered my legs into the hole and took the first step, then the next, then the next. With each step, my pulse drummed, my knees *literally* shaking. Finally, my shoes hit dirt.

Standing in a dim pool of whatever daylight was left, I turned, blinking into the blackness that surrounded me.

You've probably heard the expression, *'I could feel someone staring at me.'* That moment, I knew without question, that someone was looking at me. Staring at me. The air around me was still, the room was silent, but there was no doubt in my mind that someone, something, was there with me.

A presence.

CABIN 2 (STEELE SHADOWS SECURITY)

~

★ RATTLESNAKE ROAD ★

I am beyond excited to unveil the cover for a top secret project I've been plotting and working on for almost a year. **Rattlesnake Road**, the first book in a series of **standalone** Romantic Mysteries, is scheduled to be released in the spring of 2021. It will be my most evocative, sexy, thrilling ride yet. I CANNOT wait to give it to you.

Rattlesnake Road is up for pre-order now, so you can reserve your copy today!

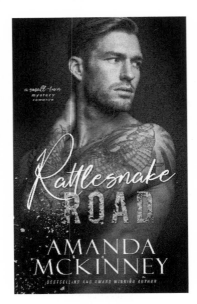

From bestselling and award-winning author Amanda McKinney comes an emotional and twisted new small-town Mystery Romance...

Everyone hits rock bottom, only the brave escape.

Welcome to 1314 Rattlesnake Road.

A quaint two-bedroom log cabin nestled deep in the woods outside the small, southern town of Berry Springs—the perfect hideaway to escape your past.

Tucked inside thick, mahogany walls lay mysterious letters, untouched, unearthed for decades. Floor-to-ceiling windows frame breathtaking views of mountains, soaring cliffs, deep valleys, and endless lies. Mature oak and pine trees speckle a rolling back yard, tall enough to carry the whispers of the haunted, of stories untold.

Inside sits Grey Dalton, emotionally battered and bruised, her only wish to pick up the broken pieces of her life. But outside, await two men, one a tattooed cowboy, the other a dashing businessman.
One will steal her heart, the other, her soul.

Rattlesnake Road is a standalone mystery romance about love, loss, hitting rock bottom, and clawing your way to the other side.

Your escape awaits...

Pre-order Today

♥ *And don't forget to sign up for my exclusive reader group and blogging team!* ♥

STEALS AND DEALS

★LIMITED TIME STEALS AND DEALS★

1. The Creek (A Berry Springs Novel), only **$0.99**
2. Bestselling and award-nominated Cabin 1 (Steele Shadows Security), **FREE**
3. Devil's Gold (A Black Rose Mystery), only **$0.99**

(1) The Creek (A Berry Springs Novel)

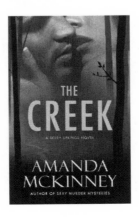

When DNA evidence links Lieutenant Quinn Colson's brother to the scene of a grisly murder, Quinn realizes he'll do anything to keep his brother from returning to prison, even if it costs him his job... and the woman who's stolen his heart.

Get The Creek today for only $0.99

(2) Cabin 1 (Steele Shadows Security)

★2020 National Readers' Choice Award Finalist, 2020 HOLT Medallion Finalist★

Hidden deep in the remote mountains of Berry Springs is a private security firm where some go to escape, and others find exactly what they've been looking for.

Welcome to Cabin 1, Cabin 2, Cabin 3...

Get Cabin 1 for ★FREE★ today

(3) Devil's Gold

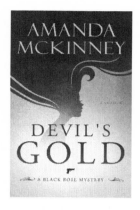

"With fast-paced action, steamy romance, and a good dose of mystery, Devil's Gold is a solid whodunit that will keep you surprised at every turn." -Siobhan Novelties

"...smart, full of energetic thrills and chills, it's one of the best novellas I've read in a very long time." -Booked J

Get Devil's Gold today for only $0.99

Sign up for my Newsletter so you don't miss out on more Steals and Deals! https://www.amandamckinneyauthor.com/contact

★Hey book lovers, book bloggers, and bookstagrammers★ Want to participate in the promo events for my books? Just go to my website to sign up! Easy squeezy!

https://www.amandamckinneyauthor.com/contact

ABOUT THE AUTHOR

Amanda McKinney is the bestselling and multi-award-winning author of more than fifteen romantic suspense and mystery novels. She wrote her debut novel, LETHAL LEGACY, after walking away from her career to become a writer and stay-at-home mom. Her books include the BERRY SPRINGS SERIES, STEELE SHADOWS SERIES, and the BLACK ROSE MYSTERY SERIES, with many more to come. Amanda lives in Arkansas with her handsome husband, two beautiful boys, and three obnoxious dogs.

Text **AMANDABOOKS to 66866** to sign up for Amanda's Newsletter and get the latest on new releases, promos, and freebies!

www.amandamckinneyauthor.com

If you enjoyed Cabin 1, please write a review!

THE AWARD-WINNING BERRY SPRINGS SERIES

The Woods (A Berry Springs Novel)
The Lake (A Berry Springs Novel)
The Storm (A Berry Springs Novel)
The Fog (A Berry Springs Novel)
The Creek (A Berry Springs Novel)
The Shadow (A Berry Springs Novel)
The Cave (A Berry Springs Novel)

#1 BESTSELLING STEELE SHADOWS

Cabin 1 (Steele Shadows Security)
Cabin 2 (Steele Shadows Security)
Cabin 3 (Steele Shadows Security)
Phoenix (Steele Shadows Rising)
Jagger (Steele Shadows Investigations)
Ryder (Steele Shadows Investigations)

★*Rattlesnake Road, coming spring 2021* ★

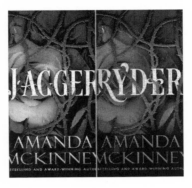

Like your sexy murder mysteries with a side of evil witch?
Check out THE BLACK ROSE MYSTERY SERIES about three
super-rich, independent, badass sisters who run a private
investigation company in a creepy, southern town...

Devil's Gold (A Black Rose Mystery, Book 1)
Hatchet Hollow (A Black Rose Mystery, Book 2)
Tomb's Tale (A Black Rose Mystery Book 3)
Evil Eye (A Black Rose Mystery Book 4)
Sinister Secrets (A Black Rose Mystery Book 5)

Made in the USA
Monee, IL
12 September 2021

77894444R00146